Pinning her shoulders down, Amanda kissed her into silence. Then, beset by an aching compulsion to be part of Debby's flesh, she found her way chaotically inside her, and they were suddenly gasping and biting and sweating as if they had only this moment to transcend their separation.

Fair Play

An Amanda Valentine Mystery

by

ROSE BEECHAM

THE NAIAD PRESS, INC.
1995

Printed in the United States of America on acid-free paper
First Edition

Editor: Christine Cassidy
Cover designer: Bonnie Liss (Phoenix Graphics)
Typesetter: Sandi Stancil

Library of Congress Cataloging-in-Publication Data

Beecham, Rose, 1958 –
    Fair play / by Rose Beecham.
        p.   cm. — (An Amanda Valentine mystery ; 3)
    ISBN 1-56280-081-7 (pbk.)
    I. Title.   II. Series: Beecham, Rose, 1958 –   Amanda Valentine
mystery ; 3.
PR9639.3.B344F35   1995
823—dc20   95-14530
                                                              CIP

Dedication

I salute my companion in crime —
the long macchiato

ABOUT THE AUTHOR

Rose Beecham is a pseudonym of Jennifer Fulton, author of *Passion Bay, Saving Grace, True Love,* and *Greener Than Grass*. A New Zealander, Jennifer divides her time between two cities — Wellington, NZ, and Melbourne, Australia. The Amanda Valentine series includes *Introducing Amanda Valentine, Second Guess* and *Fair Play*.

Books by Jennifer Fulton

PASSION BAY

SAVING GRACE

TRUE LOVE

GREENER THAN GRASS

As "Rose Beecham"

INTRODUCING AMANDA VALENTINE

SECOND GUESS

FAIR PLAY

CHAPTER ONE

The tip-off call came in at six, as the Friday evening shift was changing over.

"Bloody terrific." Detective Senior Sergeant Austin Shaw slammed down his phone in an uncharacteristic display of emotion. "I have tickets to *La Bohème*."

Tickets plural. Amanda surveyed her dark-haired colleague with interest.

"The opera." Shaw explained, taking for granted her ignorance of matters cultural. "Puccini . . . the Australian reconceptualization."

"Right." Amanda remembered seeing it in the

1

newspapers. The Australians had created a fantastically costumed Fifties interpretation of the famous opera. After touring the show to rave reviews in America and Europe, they were giving a single megabucks performance in New Zealand before heading back to Sydney. Austin Shaw looked tragic at the prospect of missing the show. "So where's the body?" Amanda asked.

"In Thorndon. Highbury Grove Apartments. Webley's on his way 'round there to seal the place off." Shaw checked his watch and picked up his phone again. "I'll call forensics."

Amanda examined the abstract photo essay on his wall. Perhaps the white blur in the center was a bird, she mused, or maybe a tennis racquet. "What have we got on the tip-off call?" she asked when he was off the phone.

"Traced it to a pay box in Lambton Quay. We've dispatched a car."

"One car?" Amanda raised critical eyebrows. At this time of night the central business district would be swarming with commuters headed for home. If the killer himself had made the tip-off call, a highly visible police presence could possibly flush him out. Guilty people tended to make themselves obvious.

"All available units are down at the French Embassy," Shaw said. "For the protest march."

The French could not have picked a worse time to announce the resumption of nuclear testing in the South Pacific, Amanda reflected. Police resources were already strained to the limit with the usual increases in shoplifting, petty theft and domestic disputes that winter inspired among people who had trouble paying their electricity bills. Who needed protesters climbing walls, burning flags and lobbing stinkbombs into ambassadorial cocktail parties?

"We've got to get some uniforms down there," she said, irritated that Shaw hadn't worked this out for himself. "Dispatch a couple of mufti cars, for goodness' sakes."

Shaw rocked back and forth in his highly polished shoes, something he did when he was impatient. Or completely preoccupied.

Amanda had a surprising thought. "Are you going with your mother?" she asked casually. "To the opera, I mean?"

Shaw met her phony disinterest without a blink. "I'm taking a friend."

"You're having a private life?" Amanda allowed herself to look gobstruck.

Unresponsive, her colleague lifted his cream trench coat from its hook. "I could get there right after the performance."

"There's no need for self-sacrifice." Amanda plucked the log sheet from his desk and scanned it. "Suspected homicide. One dead male . . . I think I can handle it." He was on a date of the hot and heavy variety, she decided. Seldom had she seen him fidgety. Shaw was the classic observer, a detective in the Sherlock Holmes mold — elegant, educated, enigmatic. Amanda could think of at least three officers who would sell their mothers for a date with him, and that was just the men.

Most of the female staff at Police Headquarters had him picked for gay, she realized. But after six years of working with him, Amanda had learned that

3

it was unwise to make assumptions about Shaw. He was a fine homicide detective and that, as far as she was concerned, was what counted.

She returned to her office to collect her satchel then followed him to the elevators, wishing she could dream up an excuse for ordering surveillance on the Opera House. Why was she so interested in whom Shaw was seeing anyway? she chided herself. Was her own private life so barren she had sunk to inventing soap operas starring friends and colleagues? Yes, a small voice needled. "No," she mumbled to herself, attracting an inquiring look from her companion.

The elevator doors opened to a wall of chill clammy air. Crossing the underground parking lot, Amanda chaffed her hands together and cursed the recent loss of her favorite kid gloves. Wellington was worse than Chicago in winter. This year the usual biting southerly winds had arrived early, defoliating every tree in the city and prompting a stampede on nasal decongestants.

"You can reach me on the mobile," Shaw hovered as Amanda's car approached.

"Go!" she said. "Fellini awaits you."

He could barely conceal a cringe. "Puccini."

"Whatever." With a nod to the uniformed constable in the driver's seat, she fastened her seat belt and delivered a cheerful wave.

Arms folded, dark eyebrows slightly gathered, Shaw watched them drive off. Amanda had no idea what he was thinking.

The victim was white, male and extremely dead.

One bullet would have been sufficient, squarely placed in the chest at close range. Two had ensured there was no mistake. Three seemed somewhat excessive.

Amanda pondered on that as she took in the upscale surroundings. Everything was cream and chrome, with dashes of some murky shade the decorator doubtless termed cappuccino. Her immediate impression was of pristine order undermined. The clues were subtle — a sideboard with all its drawers closed flush, bar one which was open a couple of centimeters, a lacquered box slightly skewed in the center of the fire surround. There were no immediate signs of struggle, forced entry or burglary. The dead man lay sprawled over the arm of a blood-soaked mint-green sofa.

"Looks like three shots at extreme close range, ma'am." Detective Sergeant Gordon Webley dragged on a pair of standard issue latex gloves.

From the victim's wounds, Amanda built a quick mental picture of the shooting. The first shot had gone straight into his chest, squarely entering the sofa behind him, the angle suggesting killer and victim were seated opposite each other. There had been left a gross wound, scorching the surrounding flesh and clothing. The second shot appeared to have been fired on a slight downward arc, probably piercing a lung. The third was quite different, entering at the base of the throat and exiting on a crossward trajectory to the right of the spine, implying a right-handed killer. It appeared the bullet had lodged in the base of an art deco-style blond oak sideboard nearby.

Amanda studied the dead man's head. His hair was bleached blond, mousy at the roots. Heavily gelled, it bore testimony to interference, a twisted clump falling over his cloudy eyes. Had the killer pulled the victim's head back to fire that final throat shot? If so, it was a highly personal act.

"Looks like our man." Webley flashed a foreign passport, adding, "Found this on the sideboard."

"An Australian." Amanda scanned the personal details. "Bryce Robin Petty. Born nineteen sixty-five."

"Hard to believe he's thirty," Webley commented. "Looks like a choirboy."

"A choirboy with a big appetite." Amanda noted the fleshy legs and arms. Not a tall man, the victim occupied that unhappy zone between flab and muscle tone. Two weeks skipping the gym and you're a blimp. Amanda could relate to that. Approaching the body, she placed a hand on the neck. "Still warm. Dead maybe a couple of hours."

Marty Nikora, one of the younger detectives on her team, entered the room. "D.C. Harrison's down on the Quay, Inspector. Nothing to report. Couple of French restaurants handing out free croissants, that's all." He surveyed the gory scene in a perfunctory manner, commenting, "Jeez, that couch is a goner."

Brilliant detection. The boy was a surefire promotion prospect. Amanda signaled him to accompany her. "C'mon, let's take a look around."

Extracting his notebook with alacrity, Nikora clumped across the polished wooden floorboards. "Never know your luck, eh," he said cheerfully. "Maybe the perp's hiding in the bathroom."

The apartment was brand new, part of a development intended for well-paid professionals who worked in the financial district just minutes from the front entrance. The walk-to-work concept was an easy sell in New Zealand where people were generally safe on the streets.

The killer was not waiting in the slate-tiled bathroom, but to Amanda's satisfaction there were traces of blood in the shower box and around the rim of the wash basin. "Looks like a Mr. Clean," she commented. Often a killer would wash hurriedly at the scene of the crime, leaving a trail of giveaway hairs and fiber. With any luck, this dude might have flushed some vital trace down the plughole, only to have it lodge in the U-bend where Moira McDougall's minions would swoop on it with their tiny tweezers.

The cupboards beneath the basin were closed. Opening them, Amanda was greeted with an avalanche of bottles and tubes — cleaning fluid, after-shave, men's cologne and various hair products.

"Looks like someone's been in there," Nikora stated the obvious.

Was the killing incidental to a burglary? Amanda doubted it. Yet she was certain the place had been searched. Removing one of her gloves, she felt the towel hanging beside the shower box. It was slightly damp, used three or four hours ago, she guessed. If the killer had helped himself to the victim's towels, he had no doubt taken them with him to dump away from the scene.

Bryce Petty was wearing sports clothing. Had he left work early, gone to the gym, returned home and disturbed an intruder? Or had he taken the day off? Presumably he had a job. You didn't run an apartment like this on welfare.

Between the bathroom and the main bedroom was a study alcove which overlooked a courtyard garden. Like the rest of the apartment, the compact workspace was disrupted by pockets of chaos. A pen carousel was overturned, its contents spilled on the desk. A filing cabinet had been rifled, and someone had disturbed the desk drawers. A red light blinked on the answer machine.

Instructing Nikora to take notes and summoning Webley to observe, as the scenes-of-crime officer, Amanda pressed the playback button to hear the uncleared messages.

There was only one. An impatient male voice. "Are you there Bryce? We have to talk. It's important. Ring me." The message time was recorded by a synthetic computer voice as 3:15 p.m.

"No name," Nikora said.

Amanda wound the tape back to the beginning, hoping that like many people, Bryce Petty did not bother to wipe old messages until his tape ran out. After a prolonged hiss, several recordings played, each with its time logged automatically.

"Wiremu here. Can you call me about tomorrow night?" 10:15 a.m.

This was followed by a message at 11:00 a.m. in the same frustrated tone they had just heard. "Bryce. This is your father. Do you hear me? If you're there, pick up the damned phone!" A pause. "Okay. Call me. I'm at the Plaza Hotel. Room six-one-nine."

The player beeped and another message began, this time a woman spoke. "Bryce. Hello? It's —" The machine beeped and returned to the 3:15 p.m. message.

"Guess he picked up the phone when that lady . . . woman called," Nikora said. "Maybe it was his girlfriend."

"So, he interrupted the answer machine and it

didn't record a time. Then, when his father called at three fifteen —"

"He could have been dead or alive," Webley said. "Sounds like he didn't want to talk to his old man."

Amanda checked the volume setting on the machine. It was turned up, enabling calls to be monitored. She envisioned Bryce Petty listening to his father but not picking up the phone. Why hadn't he reset the machine if he did not intend to respond?

"Shame we don't know what time the girlfriend phoned." Nikora contributed another of his classic understatements.

"Indeed." Amanda bagged the answer machine tape then poked around in the filing cabinet. There was nothing but some computer literature and a few manila folders full of personal papers. Shuffling through these, she noted numerous references to a company called Spectrum Television.

"Never heard of them," Nikora said.

"Looks like he worked for them in Australia." Amanda returned the papers temporarily to the cabinet. They would analyze Petty's personal documents later. For the moment their priority was to reconstruct the killing and, if possible, make an early arrest.

Taking a final glance around the study, she moved across the hallway to the main bedroom which was, by her standards anyway, spectacularly tidy.

Nikora gave a low whistle. "Swank-ee." Entering the spacious room, he gazed around in apparent awe, then pointed at a cardboard-framed snapshot on the dresser. "Hey, get this."

The photograph, apparently taken in a restaurant, showed Petty sitting opposite a tall, powerfully built

9

Maori man whose face seemed vaguely familiar. Mentally scrolling mugshots, Amanda cast an inquiring glance at her companion. "You know this guy?"

Nikora made a poor job of concealing his incredulity. "Ma'am, that's Wiremu Awatere, the rugby player — All Black reserve in the 'ninety-five World Cup side. Should have played in the final. Then we might have beaten South Africa."

"Looks like he was friends with the deceased." Amanda turned the picture over, looking for the processing date. "Taken three weeks ago." Bagging it, she instructed Nikora to remove the top drawer from the dresser and place it on the bed.

The contents seemed fairly typical for a young bachelor. Keys, dockets, a bulk bag of condoms, a pump pack of lubricant and an inlaid wooden box which held a few items of jewelry.

"Nice ring." Nikora admired a thick gold band set with a cabochon ruby. "Guy must have been making a buck." Subjecting the room to another sweeping glance, he added with faint chagrin, "I s'pose the ladies really go for this kind of thing, eh?"

Amanda took in the pale gray painted wood and angular black light fittings, the meaningless abstract paintings in narrow metal frames. The room was full of sharp edges, its aesthetic self-consciously ultra-modern. There were no books, no used coffee mugs on the black bedside tables, no clutter on the surfaces. A lingering hint of lemon-scented furniture wax suggested the place had been professionally cleaned in the past few days. Mentally making a note to trace Petty's cleaning service, she remarked, "Doesn't do a thing for me."

"You're a cop, ma'am." Nikora's tone was dismissive.

"As opposed to a 'lady'?"

With a wry grimace, Nikora backed off. "Shall I go look in the kitchen, Inspector?"

Amanda slid the drawer back into the dresser. "Sure. But don't eat anything." Unmoved by an affronted glower from her subordinate, she returned her attention to the search.

Nikora loathed to be reminded of past misdeeds, but they had a habit of following him from one assignment to the next. He was a promising young detective, the pride and joy of the CIB's rugby team — a fact which had earned him the chief's undying gratitude but cut no ice with Amanda. He was exactly the kind of hothead who, convinced he was infallible, would make stupid mistakes.

Initially she had been reluctant to keep him on her team, but the kid had a freshness and enthusiasm that often paid dividends in the complex casework the CIB handled. Nikora never shirked the dull slog that made up a huge part of any homicide investigation. He could be relied on to offer up new theories, no matter how farfetched they seemed. And every now and then he came up with a hunch that paid off.

Amanda flicked through a packet of photographs she had unearthed in Petty's bottom drawer. Taken the previous year, they were mostly run-of-the-mill scenic snaps — the Cook Strait Ferry chugging across tranquil Wellington Harbour, views of a rocky stretch of beach that looked like Breaker Bay. Among the beach photos were several of Awatere, the rugby player, reclining in tiny bathing trunks.

11

Trying to avoid drawing conclusions, she studied the contents of Bryce Petty's top drawer once again. So many condoms, yet so little evidence of any female presence in the victim's life, apart from the unidentified woman whose voice they'd heard on the answer machine.

"Ma'am?" Nikora appeared in the doorway. "Found something in the laundry."

Amanda followed him through the living area where David Wong, the police photographer, was perched on a step ladder, his camera trained on the body. Blinking against the glare of the lights, Amanda acknowledged a couple of pallid young pathologists from Moira McDougall's forensic team. Their boss wouldn't be far away, she guessed. Moira always hurried for a warm corpse.

"It's in there." Nikora pointed to a dark garment soaking in the laundry tub.

Amanda peered into the murky water, unable to discern any sign that the garment was bloodied. Nikora fished it out and held it aloft, his expression reverential. It was a black football jersey bearing a white fern leaf on the front and a number on the back.

"An All Black jersey, right?" Amanda surmised.

"It's Awatere's number." Nikora lowered the hallowed garment back into the suds, adding without conviction, "Must have given it to this Petty guy."

"You think so?"

Nikora looked uneasy. "The guys are always swapping jerseys with teams they play."

"You think our Mr. Petty looks like a football player?"

"Stocky build. Could be a winger."

"Too much flab," Webley contributed from the adjoining room.

"I think Mr. Awatere may be able to help us with our inquiries," Amanda told a flabbergasted Nikora. "Pick him up."

"We can't do that," Nikora croaked. "How's it gonna look if a cop car turns up at Wiremu Awatere's place and takes him away? It'll be all over the tele."

Amanda raised her eyebrows. "He's not O.J. Simpson."

"No, ma'am." Nikora vehemently endorsed this sentiment. "Awatere's a *real* hero. He'd never —"

"Did I say we were arresting him?" Amanda stemmed the adulation. "Use a mufti car if you want. I don't care. Just get Awatere downtown. I'll interview him when I'm done here."

Nikora's face was mournful. "He didn't do it," he doggedly informed her.

"Then he has nothing to worry about," she said coolly.

CHAPTER TWO

Back at Police Headquarters an hour later, Amanda had barely removed her coat when a tall woman with coppery hair and very pink cheeks stuck her head around the door.

"Harrison?" Amanda felt a pang of unease. At one time the junior detective had nursed an embarrassing crush on her, an unrequited passion Amanda had firmly squashed. Harrison had since got herself a love life, but she was still awkward around Amanda, presumably the legacy of baring her soul only to be rejected.

Avoiding Amanda's eyes, she said stiffly, "Sorry to disturb you, ma'am. I . . . need some advice."

"Uh huh?" Amanda shuffled some papers, wishing she could defuse the tension that prickled whenever she and Harrison were in the same room.

"It's about a friend." Harrison gnawed on her lower lip. "Something awful's happened. I don't know where to start!" With that, she burst into tears and, mumbling an incoherent apology, began backing toward the door.

"Hang on a minute." Amanda got to her feet and crossed the room, taking the young woman firmly by the arm and installing her in a chair. "What's the problem, here?" She could hardly bear to listen. Harrison's girlfriend had probably dumped her and now she would need six months of therapy to get a life again. On the job, she'd be a cot-case — introspective, sullen and sexually frustrated.

"You know my girlfriend, Anya?" Harrison blurted. "Well, it's her flatmate."

Terrific. The girlfriend bonks the flatmate and Harrison finds out about it. Maybe she walked in on them. Amanda glanced at her watch. She really didn't have time for this. Nikora had called to say they'd picked up Awatere and were on their way downtown.

"It's just terrible." Harrison sniffed. "Anya got home a couple of hours ago and found her tied up in the kitchen. She nearly fainted."

Amanda leaned against her desk craving a strong coffee. "Tied up? What are we talking about?"

15

"Sexual violation," Harrison said in a choked voice.

"You're saying the flatmate's been raped?"

"Anya thinks so. But Sara won't talk about it."

Amanda was silent. Hers was a homicide unit. Sexual violation was handled by the rape squad unless a serial attacker was suspected, or unless there was evidence of an attempted homicide. "You want me to talk to someone about this?"

Harrison shook her head. "No. I was hoping... Sara told Anya not to call the police. She's upset."

"The rape squad won't touch this without a statement."

"That's why I'm talking to you. Please," Harrison implored. "Can't we just make a few routine inquiries?"

"You want me to approve an informal investigation?" Surely Harrison was not that naïve. "You know that's not possible. If the victim doesn't want the police involved —"

"Maybe she'd listen to you!"

"I can't imagine why."

"Because you're famous and women respect you." Harrison was the stereotypical stubborn redhead. "Please."

Amanda focused on the muted sound of telephones ringing, a constant background din at Police Headquarters. "I can't."

"You mean you won't!" Janine Harrison got to her feet so abruptly her chair toppled over. "Sara's only eighteen. She's confused."

"Then I suggest you call the Rape Crisis Center and arrange some counseling for her." Conflicting emotions stirred Amanda's insides. A few years ago, she might have burdened herself with a no-hope case like this one just to see if she could make a difference. But she no longer had the energy. Meeting Harrison's wrathful stare, she reiterated as calmly as she could, "I will not resource a case we have no chance of prosecuting."

Harrison looked completely disillusioned. "It wouldn't be the first time."

Amanda controlled an urge to tell her to learn some respect, only she was right. The department thought nothing of pouring resources into half-baked undercover drug operations, but rape investigations were way down on the glamor scale, unlikely to attract citations, overseas trips or unlimited overtime. *Stay out of it,* she told herself. "Has she washed?" she asked Harrison, thinking, *Sucker.*

The young detective promptly wiped the tears from her face. "No. I told Anya to sit with her until we arrive."

"You did, huh?" Amanda pulled on her coat. "Remind me who's in charge here, Harrison?"

Her junior colleague gave a sheepish smile. "We both serve the public interest, ma'am."

Sara Hart looked more like a child than a woman. Just starting out. Containing a rush of futile anger, Amanda pulled a chair close to the bed and said, "Sara. My name's Amanda Valentine. I'm a friend of Janine's."

Sara opened her eyes. Her face was discolored,

17

lips swollen and bloodied. Normally she was pretty, Amanda thought. Nothing glamorous — just fresh and appealing.

"I'm sorry," Sara whispered.

"There's nothing to be sorry for." Amanda found herself swallowing a lump in her throat. Carefully she took Sara's hand. The slender wrists had been bound, and Sara had obviously struggled, the seesawing of the rope causing deep abrasions. "Sara, I want to help."

Sara stared vacantly ahead.

Amanda stroked her injured hand. "You don't have to do anything you don't want to do." Heartened to detect a faint nod, she added, "Is there someone I can call for you . . . your mom, maybe?"

Again the blank stare. Sara shook her head.

Uneasy about her pallor and the dilation of her pupils, Amanda went to the door and summoned Harrison, telling her to call a police doctor.

"But she doesn't want to see a doctor," Harrison protested.

"She's in no fit state to know what she wants." Amanda said sharply. "She's in shock, and who knows what internal injuries she might have. Now call Dr. Rosenberg, and tell your girlfriend to make a cup of very sweet tea."

She returned to the bed and, acting on impulse, pulled back the covers and wrapped the young woman in a thick quilt. Then she picked her up, carried her across the room and occupied a large armchair. Arranging Sara on her knee so that she was comfortably supported, she rocked her gently back and forth.

"You're going to be okay, Sara," she said. "I'll

look after you and I won't let anything bad happen to you."

A few minutes later, she glanced up, conscious of Harrison and her girlfriend standing in the doorway.

"We've made the tea." Harrison approached with a pottery mug. Her expression was oddly pinched.

"Give me half an hour," Amanda said. "Sara and I are talking."

"Well?" Harrison demanded as soon as they'd turned out of the driveway onto Aro Street.

"She's a mess." Amanda had taken her own notes as Dr. Rosenberg made her examination. Sara Hart had been gagged and blindfolded, beaten, burned with cigarettes, bitten and raped.

After the examination, Dr. Rosenberg took Amanda aside. "I can't detect obvious traces of semen, but I've taken extra swabs. The lab will turn up something."

It was uncommon, but not unheard of for semen to be absent from a rape. Fearing DNA tests, some perpetrators used condoms or tried to avoid ejaculation. The bite marks were something, Amanda thought. The doctor had scraped for saliva. At least that would link the perp to a blood group.

"She's agreed to give me a statement tomorrow," Amanda told Harrison as they returned to the city. "It happened in the house — the living room. I want you to get back there tonight with a couple of Moira's boys. Print everything, get whatever trace you can. I want to nail this creep."

* * * * *

Nikora and Wiremu Awatere appeared to be deep in conversation when Amanda entered the interview room.

Nikora stood instantly. "We were talking about South Africa, ma'am. Wiremu met Mr. Mandela."

"I'm happy for you." Amanda introduced herself and asked Awatere if he knew why they wanted to talk with him.

The animation seeped from the footballer's expression. "The detective here told me about Bryce."

"And that's the first you knew of your friend Mr. Petty's death?"

Awatere exchanged a glance with Nikora.

Wondering what else the uneasy-looking detective had discussed with his hero, Amanda said, "Have you informed Mr. Awatere of his rights?"

Both men seemed to flinch at her tone.

"Yes, ma'am," Nikora said.

"You understand this conversation is being recorded?" Amanda's stomach rumbled as she sat down. She should have picked up a burger on her way back to the station but all she could think about was Sara Hart shivering against her.

"Look," Wiremu Awatere said in an undertone, "I need to keep this thing quiet, Inspector. The team just signed this deal with Rupert Murdoch . . ."

"You haven't answered my question," Amanda said crisply.

"I didn't do anything." Awatere groaned.

"Do you deny telephoning us from a phone booth in Lambton Quay at six tonight to report the killing of a Mr. Bryce Petty?" Amanda injected her voice with a brazen conviction intended to disguise the truth — that they had precisely zilch to connect Awatere with the tip-off call.

"I knew it." Awatere choked. "I knew you'd find out. Jesus, I can't go anywhere. I suppose it was that kid I gave the autograph to."

Amanda was silent. Some subjects dug their own graves. All you had to do was offer them a shovel and get out of the way.

"Oh shit, man." Burying his head in his hands, Awatere asked, "Do I need a lawyer?"

"You're not charged with anything," Amanda said, reluctant to have him lawyer up too quickly. "But I can have D.C. Nikora caution you once more if you're not certain about your rights."

"No. I understand." Awatere wiped away a trickle of perspiration that was rolling down his temple. His breathing was uneven. Shakily, he accepted a glass of water Nikora poured for him. "I found him," he admitted. "Fucking hell. I didn't know what to do. It's not easy, y'know."

"Finding a body?" Amanda tried to sound sympathetic. Her stomach gurgled audibly. Nearly ten o'clock and all she'd eaten since breakfast was a limp Danish pastry and a few vitamin C pills.

"You gotta keep your nose clean," Awatere went on, bleakly self-absorbed. "Keep the sponsors happy. Man, it was my dream . . . wearing the colors. Ever since I was a kid, I wanted to be an All Black."

You're breaking my heart, Amanda thought. "How long had you known Bryce Petty?" she asked.

"Met him in Melbourne last year when we were

playing the Wallabies." Awatere's eyes wandered. "He moved over here a few weeks back. We had a few drinks . . ."

Amanda could sense Nikora's astonishment. Apparently sharing the occasional beer was not the kind of mateship that warranted the gift of a coveted All Black football jersey.

"You found Mr. Petty dead," Amanda said. "How did you get into his apartment?"

Awatere hesitated. "I had a key. I was staying there a few days last week."

That could explain the football jersey soaking in the laundry, Amanda supposed, and account for any fingerprints. Noting Nikora's premature relief, she fired a warning glance at him and continued in a tone of outright disbelief. "Don't you have your own house, Mr. Awatere?"

Awatere fidgeted. "I needed some time out. The media won't leave us alone, ever since we got back from the tour. Bryce said I could stay at his place. Y'know, lay low for a few days."

Amanda responded with abject scorn. "And you kept the key? How convenient."

"I forgot about it!" Awatere was rattled. "I was going to give it back today. That's how come I found him. I didn't —"

"Do you make a habit of carrying the keys to other men's apartments, Mr. Awatere?" Amanda cut in silkily.

His response was not the blustering denial she expected. Instead he lowered his head. "I didn't kill him," he half-whispered.

"What time did you arrive at Mr. Petty's apartment?"

"About five-thirty." Awatere poured some more water into his glass. His hand shook.

Sensing he was the kind of subject who would clam up under pressure, Amanda softened her confrontational tone slightly. "Can you remember if anyone saw you enter or leave the apartment?"

"There were some people on the street, but I didn't really look at them." He sounded regretful. "You gotta prove what I'm saying, right?"

"The sooner we know everything, the sooner we can eliminate you from our inquiries," Amanda said. "Tell me about this afternoon. What were you doing before you went to Mr. Petty's place?"

Awatere was positively eager. Wednesday was a training day, he said. This morning he'd started with three hours' swimming at the Kilbirnie Aquatic Centre. Then he saw his physio about an injury to his ankle. Afterwards, he did a charity lunch with a sports reporter from TV3, and when he'd finished pressing the flesh he worked out in the Les Mills gym until around five. There were at least a hundred people who could vouch for his whereabouts at different times of the day.

With a flourish, Nikora took down a list of names.

"And after you left the gym, you went straight to Mr. Petty's apartment . . . was he expecting you?"

Awatere hesitated. "I said I might drop 'round for a beer."

"When did you tell him that?"

"Bryce rang me at the gym, about two o'clock."

"Did he say where he was calling from?"

"Must have been at home. He said he got my message on the answer machine."

"And he invited you over. Did he suggest a time?"

"Five o'clock."

"Tell me about finding him. Did you touch him?"

Awatere shook his head vehemently. "No way. I was out of there, man. I knew I had to ring you guys, so . . ."

"You declined to give your name," Amanda said. "That is exactly the kind of behavior that causes suspicion, Mr. Awatere."

Awatere cradled his forehead. "The coach is gonna kill me. You don't know what it's like. There's the sponsors and my *whanau*. I'm a role model for Maori kids, Inspector. They look up to me." He seemed close to tears.

Amanda considered her options. Awatere wasn't behaving like a man with murder on his conscience, but then neither had Ted Bundy. Although she was becoming uneasily certain that he was not their perpetrator, she was equally sure he was more than a mere drinking buddy of Petty's. On an impulse, she suspended the interview, instructing Nikora. "Go get some coffee for Mr. Awatere."

As the door closed behind him, she flicked off the tape and, leaning a little closer to her subject, said quietly, "You're not on tape now, Mr. Awatere. So, any information you give me is off the record. Am I right in guessing you were Bryce Petty's lover?"

Awatere stared at the table.

"You can make this hard for yourself. Or can help me and I'll do my best to keep your name out of the tabloids."

Awatere clenched and unclenched his fists. "Okay," he admitted. "He was my boyfriend."

"Did this start when you met him in Melbourne?"

"Yeah. And he came over for a holiday last Christmas —"

There was a knock at the door and Nikora entered carrying a tray of coffee and biscuits. As he poured a cup for Awatere, Amanda considered the direction her questioning should take. Technically Awatere was a prime suspect. The time of death had not been established, and he had admitted to being at the scene between five-thirty and quarter to six. But at this stage it was not essential to expose him on tape as the dead man's lover. He was cooperating and there seemed little to be gained by outing him.

She hesitated for a moment, questioning her professional judgment. The relationship between the two men was undoubtably important to get on record, but Awatere's desire to conceal it could be a useful bargaining chip. "You have a clean record, Mr. Awatere," she said. "We can understand a person panicking in your situation. But we need your complete cooperation if we're going to find the person who committed this crime. For a start, we'd like to take your fingerprints and run a couple of tests for gunpowder."

Awatere looked almost keen. "Help yourself."

Watching Nikora assemble the nitrate test and prints kit, Amanda asked, "Do you have any idea who might have had a reason to kill your friend Mr. Petty?"

Awatere shrugged. "Bryce didn't know too many people over here."

"Did he ever speak about his father?"

"Sometimes." Awatere allowed his right thumb to be inked. "They didn't get on too good. His old man is big in the church."

"Had Bryce seen him recently?"

"Doubt it. He said the old man didn't know where he was."

"That's odd. He phoned Bryce today."

Awatere seemed surprised by this, and even more perplexed when Amanda mentioned the female caller. Bryce didn't have a girlfriend, he assured her, but there was an older sister who lived up North. They didn't get on either. She was, according to Bryce, a real bitch.

Amanda collected her thoughts. You couldn't fire three bullets into someone at close range without being splattered with blood. If Awatere was the killer he must have changed his clothing and showered, possibly leaving a trail of forensic evidence in his car and house. "What clothing were you wearing when you went into Mr. Petty's apartment?" she asked.

Awatere stared down at his jeans and sweater. "These."

"Tell me what happened when you let yourself in. You opened the door and entered the hall. Then what?"

Awatere consulted the ceiling. "I called out his name."

"And then?"

Awatere gazed at the intricate smudges on the prints card. "He didn't answer."

"The front door was definitely locked when you arrived?"

"Yeah. It locks automatically. You can open it from the inside without a key, but not from the outside."

"So you entered the sitting room?"

Awatere mopped his face with his sleeve. "I saw the blood . . . round the side of the couch . . . then him. Man I thought I was going to spew, so I went in the bathroom and splashed my face. I was a mess. Fucking hands were shaking like crazy."

"Did you use a towel?" Amanda asked without inflection.

"Yeah. Got one from under the basin. All this stuff fell out, but I put it back in the cupboard."

"Where is the towel you used?"

Awatere looked blank for a moment. "Must be in the car."

Amanda could picture the action exactly as he described it. A panic-stricken football star finds his lover murdered. Desperate to hide their relationship, he flees the scene as quickly as possible. Logically, if Awatere had killed Petty, he would have removed any items which connected him to the dead man. Someone had turned the place over. If it wasn't Awatere, it was probably the killer. Amanda wondered what had been taken. "Did you notice anything missing from the apartment?" she asked.

"I don't remember."

"How would you feel about taking a look around the place for us?" Amanda was aware most Maori people were reluctant, without the appropriate rituals, to enter a place where a death had recently occurred or where a body lay. This was considered *tapu,* or sacred, in their culture. Trying to show some sensitivity, she added, "After they've taken the body away."

This failed to reassure Awatere. "No way," he said.

Abandoning that possibility for the moment, Amanda said, "We'll need the clothes you're wearing and that towel from your car. D.C. Nikora will escort you home to change into something else." She helped herself to one of the chocolate biscuits on the tray. "Oh, and also," she added, like it was some casual afterthought, "we'd like to take a look around your place. Is that okay with you?"

Awatere was silent, his dark eyes appealing. Shuffling forward, he whispered hoarsely, "Please . . . I've got these magazines and videos . . . of men."

"I see." Closing the interview and turning off the tape, Amanda glanced at Nikora. "It seems Mr. Awatere is worried about some pornographic material he has in his house. I think it would be a good idea if he handed this over to the Indecent Publications Tribunal while the amnesty is operating."

Nikora made a poor job of concealing a smirk.

With a quelling glance, Amanda said, "There's nothing funny about the exploitation of women, Nikora. In fact —" her tone became severe — "I'll attend to this matter myself. We don't want *Debby Does Dallas* turning up in the staff canteen again, do we?"

As they escorted Awatere from the interview room to the basement parking lot, Nikora said, "That was two years ago, ma'am."

Amanda smiled faintly. "I'm glad to see you're still donating money to the Rape Crisis Center after all this time."

"How'd you know about that?" Nikora looked nonplussed.

"I know everything about my team," Amanda lied blandly. "You especially, Nikora." Keeping a straight face, she got into the car after Awatere. It did no harm to let the junior staff believe she was watching them. A little paranoia was good for discipline.

CHAPTER THREE

"Well that was a waste of time," Amanda remarked as she and Nikora returned to Police Headquarters.

"I told you he didn't do it," Nikora said.

"It's too soon to determine that."

"We didn't find a thing. No gun. No blood. Nothing —"

"So he went somewhere else to clean up," Amanda said. "He used someone else's car. You know the score, Nikora. Make no assumptions." They passed some golden arches. She glanced longingly back.

"Wanna stop?" Nikora braked.

"No. I'll get something later."

He looked sideways at her. "You on a diet?"

Give me strength, Amanda thought. "Not every woman is obsessed with her weight, Nikora."

"No, ma'am." He raced the changing traffic lights. "It's just . . . you've been looking skinny lately. So, I thought . . ."

Amanda could scarcely believe she was having this conversation with a junior male colleague. She watched a flock of gulls squabbling over some festering tidbit on the harbor front. Skinny. No one had ever called her that in her life.

Back at the station, a handful of detectives milled about in the inquiry center, their expectations raised by Awatere's early detention.

"I hate to disappoint everyone," Amanda said. "But we don't have an arrest. So, let's see what we've got." Taking a felt pen, she started writing on the whiteboard, summarizing as she went. "The deceased was an Australian citizen — apparently unemployed — only been in New Zealand for six weeks. He was shot in his apartment three times at close range between two and six this afternoon. There was no sign of forced entry, so it's possible Mr. Petty knew his killer and let him in. The weapon used was a thirty-eight caliber revolver — no sign of it yet. We have one neighbor, a Mrs. Carsen, who reports seeing a white Mitsubishi sedan accelerating along Highbury Grove around three."

Detective Janine Harrison waved a freckled hand.

"Ma'am, we have a possible second sighting of that motor vehicle. A man in the block across the road saw a white Mitsubishi entering the parking bay at two-thirty. He also heard a noise he thought might have been shots, but he was watching Ricki Lake, so he didn't check it out."

Nikora guffawed. "Don't tell me . . . my sister's husband wants to adopt my stepmother . . ."

"Anything on the driver?" Amanda asked.

"White male. Black hair and sunglasses."

Amanda promptly conjured up an image of Elvis Presley. Very helpful. The human mind had no equal. "As you know we've established the identity of our tip-off caller. You should all have a transcript of Mr. Awatere's statement. So far he has cooperated with us. I don't think he's our perp, but let's not make assumptions. In his statement, Mr. Awatere claims he did not touch the deceased, but he admits he washed his hands in the bathroom. We found traces of blood around the basin rim and the shower box, however there were no visible traces on the towel he claims to have used."

She glanced toward Brody and Bergman. As usual, the two detectives were sitting together, each closely mirroring the other's body language. Originally provincial cops, they had been promoted to the CIB the previous year, joining Amanda's team after completing their training. Finding common ground in their small-town roots, aversion to coarse language and tragic faith in the justice system, they had soon fallen in together and were generally regarded as a double act.

"You've made contact with the deceased's father?" Amanda directed her question to Sandra Brody.

"Yes, ma'am." Brody was instantly on her feet, Tony Bergman a split second later. They stared down at their notebooks. "We entered the Plaza Hotel at twenty hundred hours." Brody delivered her usual prosaic report. "The deceased's father was located in the brasserie. We arranged for a member of staff to escort him to his room. There D.C. Bergman informed him of the situation."

"How did Mr. Petty handle that?" Amanda wished she had been present, but Awatere had seemed a hotter prospect at the time.

With a glance toward Brody, Bergman responded. "He appeared to be distressed by the news, ma'am."

"We've arranged for him to identify the body tomorrow morning before the autopsy," Brody added.

"I'd like to be present for that," Amanda said. "If Mr. Petty is up to it, I'll interview him then." Turning to Detective Sergeant Solomon, she asked "How's the door-knock going?"

"Female at number twelve saw a guy fitting Awatere's description getting into a car near the Highbury block around five-forty."

"Which corroborates his story," Amanda said. "Mr. Awatere says he spoke to the deceased on the phone at two this afternoon. Between that time and three-fifteen Mr. Petty took a call from an unidentified woman. She may have been the last person to speak to him, apart from the killer. We need to trace that woman and every individual who has had contact with Mr. Petty since he arrived in Wellington six weeks ago. D.S. Shaw will handle assignments tomorrow morning."

Nikora raised his hand. "Ma'am ... about that lady on the answer machine. I saw this movie called

Fatal Attraction. There was this crazy woman stalking Michael Douglas —"

"Presumably she was desperate." Amanda gathered up her papers, signaling the briefing was over.

"I just thought . . ." Nikora persisted.

"This is Wellington, New Zealand." Amanda said mildly. "Not Universal Studios."

It was midnight when Amanda got home. A crescent moon cloaked in dense cloud cover did little to alleviate the darkness, and to make matters worse the street lamp that usually lit her narrow right-of-way had fused in a storm two nights ago. The council hadn't fixed it yet.

Muttering curses, Amanda stared into the foggy void that swallowed all hundred and thirty-two concrete steps leading down to her gate. Home to a flourishing ecosystem of weeds, mosses and snails, they were steep and, in several places, dangerously cracked.

Debby had told her to get a handyman in, but Amanda had deluded herself into thinking that she would herself perform the elementary tasks of weed-spraying and patching broken concrete one fortuitous summer afternoon. Grasping the iron hand-rail, she commenced the perilous climb down, promising herself that she would call someone tomorrow.

Her neighbors' porch light was out, the husband presumably home after another evening swilling beer with his buddies. Who could blame him, she found herself thinking as she passed their house. She wouldn't hurry home to a wife like his, either. They richly deserved each other — the faded cheerleader with her constant put-downs and demands for wrought iron garden furniture, and the onetime football jock, now gone to seed. They had two repulsive children who periodically hung over Amanda's fence firing their father's discarded beer cans at Madam, who would hiss at them from a disdainful distance.

Amanda called to the little cat and was greeted with a raucous cry protesting her failure to keep regular feeding hours. Not inclined toward exertion, Madam was waiting on the bottom step. She sashayed ahead of Amanda to the front door, purring with expectation. In the kitchen, her empty feeding dish lay overturned in the middle of the linoleum, a measure of her disgust.

"I won't be held to ransom by a cat," Amanda said, spooning pet food into the bowl. "Especially one from the animal shelter." She set down the pungent meal, thankful she was not one of those tragic people who anthropomorphized their pets.

The temptation was understandable. Even she felt an occasional pang of loneliness living by herself in a large airy house which had obviously been built for a family. But most of the time she relished the solitude and tranquility.

Grabbing a piece of leftover cheesecake, she turned up the heating and wandered into her sitting room. She enjoyed sitting in her favorite armchair near the windows, with the lights off, watching the moon float above Evans Bay. Tonight her windows were misted over, and even when she wiped clear a slippery peephole, she could see nothing beyond the trees a few feet away.

Disgruntled, she turned on her messages.

"Hello, Ms. Valentine," greeted a syrupy voice. "This is Lorelle, at Dixon Dental Surgery, with a message in the interests of your dental health. Delay is the mother of decay. Please call us tomorrow to arrange for your six month checkup. 'Bye now."

Amanda forced down another mouthful of cheese-cake. She could almost feel her cavities expanding. The next message belonged to that species most cherished by the owners of answer machines — the "hi, it's me" call. "Amanda. Hi. It's me. About the party . . . what? No, I will not speak to that deadshit again. Tell him to piss off. Sorry, I'm here still. Um . . . about the party on Friday. I hope you're still coming . . . I said no! You what? You let him in here? *Hiss.* Hi. Sorry about that. New receptionist. You can bring someone if you want. To the party I mean. I don't know if Debby's back from Rwanda but even if she isn't . . . you know what I mean. Call me tomorrow."

Amanda was in no immediate danger of forgetting Roseanne's birthday party. Her best friend phoned almost every day to remind her. She wished she could work up some enthusiasm but instead found herself inventing implausible excuses not to go.

Roseanne's gatherings invariably attracted four species of women — academics, social workers, conspiracy theorists and recovered substance abusers. There was always someone who couldn't make it because they'd just taken an overdose . . . or maybe government agents had made it look that way. Everybody talked politics. The cute girls were all with someone else.

Amanda adjusted her chair to the recline position

and closed her eyes. She'd never been a party animal anyway. She preferred an intimate dinner with a woman in a tight dress. Followed by sex. Followed by a kiss goodbye and no melodramas — in other words, what she had with Debby Daley. Since their brief, torrid affair two years ago, common sense had transcended reckless passion and they now saw each other when it fitted in with their work.

Debby, whose current affairs show *The Debby Daley Hour* topped the ratings most weeks, was based an eight-hour drive away, in Auckland. She came down to the capital city if she had a political story to cover and usually stayed with Amanda. They had permission to see other people.

Amanda pictured Debby on the sofa, where she liked to curl up with a book. Her stomach immediately hollowed and she headed for the kitchen. That was another thing she missed about Debby, apart from her smell and her warm silky skin — her cooking.

Amanda inspected the refrigerator shelves. How old was the leftover combination fried rice? She sniffed it. Too old. Discarding it in the trash, she took a can of baked beans from the pantry, tipped the contents onto a plate and put it in the microwave. She didn't really feel like beans. In fact, she didn't know what she felt like.

She thought about Sara Hart again. It had been oddly comforting to hold another human being, even under those dreadful circumstances. Listening to the whoosh and spin of the microwave, Amanda closed her eyes and reflected on her craving for human touch. Sometimes it seemed she had always felt this way. Even after five years with her first lover, Kelly, she couldn't get enough of her. Perhaps she had sensed something, Amanda thought. Perhaps a presentiment of Kelly's death had prompted that niggling insecurity.

Kelly used to laugh about it, get annoyed by it, wonder when Amanda would stop behaving as if she might never get to see her again. Was that how love should be? Amanda wondered. Roseanne, who therapized her for nothing every time they had dinner, said her anxieties stemmed from her parents' divorce. Amanda had never resolved her sense of betrayal and loss after her mother left them. Then Kelly had been killed. How simple it sounded.

Amanda sprinkled grated cheese on her baked beans. She was an emotional cripple, according to Roseanne who believed that therapy was the answer — plastic surgery for the psyche. Get rid of your unsightly scars today!

Again Amanda contemplated the party. There was no way out. Perhaps she could go for an hour then leave, ostensibly on an emergency call. She chewed on a claggy mouthful of beans. Roseanne would never buy it. The beans left a chemical aftertaste in her mouth. Abandoning them on the kitchen bench, she went upstairs and turned on the shower.

Debby had insisted on redecorating her bathroom a few months back. Now, instead of clichéd Seventies woodgrain and psychedelic wallpaper, it was all chrome and white tiles with a bottle green trim. Tiny lights illuminated the floor and the shower box rim like emergency exit lighting along the aisles of an airplane. The bath was oval and very deep. Amanda preferred to use it when she could share with Debby.

She turned up the shower, relishing the sensation

of her body being steam-cleaned. No doubt Debby would start on the bedroom next. She had written from Rwanda envisioning a balcony, leisurely summer breakfasts overlooking glittering Evans Bay, dolphins chasing colorful yachts, the sky a ravishing South Pacific blue. She'd sounded homesick. Amanda wondered if that was a good thing.

Toweling herself dry, she pulled on the burgundy silk pajamas Debby had given her on her last birthday. They seemed larger than they had a month ago when she'd last worn them. In fact all her clothing had felt loose lately. Perplexed, she dragged the scale out of the cupboard and got on for the first time in a year. The reading was wrong. A hundred and twenty pounds. Normally she was one-thirty. She jiggled the settings and tried again, with the same result. In the mirror her face struck her as different, the jaw and cheekbones more prominent than usual, the gray eyes oddly shadowed. It wasn't just her new haircut, the bleached blond thinned out to reveal more of her natural ash color. Feeling uneasy, she switched off the bathroom light and got into bed. She checked her breasts for lumps. Poked around her liver and appendix. Took her pulse rate. Stared up into the darkness.

Madam purred from the empty side where Debby liked to sleep. Amanda turned on her side and tried to recreate their last lovemaking. Goosebumps crept across her breasts and thighs. Somewhere in the chilly night a dog howled. Me too, she thought.

CHAPTER FOUR

Jim Petty was in his mid-fifties. Squat and solid, he looked not unlike his son. What was left of his hair was brushed forward to mask a shiny freckled pate, the thinness on top contrasting with dense sideburns and mustache. He wore a good quality dark suit and a white shirt. His tie was butter yellow with a fine red thread. Two rings decorated his left hand — a plain wedding band and a heavy gold signet ring with a tiny diamond in the center.

His handshake was firm, and he waited for Amanda to seat herself before taking the chair she indicated. He angled his chair slightly toward Austin Shaw who was, it appeared, the person he expected he would be speaking to.

Amanda thanked him for coming to the station and impressed on him that they would handle this as quickly as possible. "Detective Senior Sergeant Shaw will explain your rights," she said.

Jim Petty found this hard to accept, his expression growing in hostility as Shaw informed him their interview would be recorded. "I am appalled," he blustered. "My son is dead, and you're treating me like a common criminal. Don't you people have any decency?"

Amanda tried to look like she hadn't heard it all before. "Mr. Petty," she soothed. "We want to catch the person who killed your son, and that means finding out as much as we can as quickly as we can. We are required by law to explain your rights."

Mr. Petty removed a white handkerchief from his breast pocket and blew his nose loudly. Little wonder he had burst veins, Amanda thought. Dragging her gaze away from his discolored face, she referred to her notes. "Could you tell me when you last spoke to your son?"

Jim Petty extracted a diary from his jacket and flicked through the pages. "I placed two calls to Bryce yesterday, one at ten in the morning and one at after three in the afternoon. He did not answer either, but I left messages on his machine." His wiry eyebrows knitted together. "Does that mean my son was lying there dead when I called?"

"As yet we haven't pinpointed a time of death," Austin Shaw said.

"I nearly went there, you know." Petty's voice

41

sounded thin. "I had a feeling something was wrong. It was completely irrational." Intuition did not rate highly with Mr. Petty, it seemed.

"Did your son return your calls?" Amanda asked.

Petty gave a cynical snort. "I didn't really expect him to. We'd had an argument, you see." Responding to Amanda's murmured encouragement, he explained, "Just a family matter — nothing to do with this dreadful business."

"Could you explain, please."

The request was clearly unwelcome but Petty seemed to think the better of avoiding it. "If you must know, my son had something in his possession that my wife is ridiculously attached to. We wanted to get it back." He folded his arms. "It's silly. An old clock that doesn't even keep time."

Amanda tried to recall the clocks in Bryce Petty's apartment. There was only one and it looked brand new. "I don't recall seeing such a clock at your son's apartment," she said.

Petty shrugged. "He probably sold it." There was an incongruous flicker of satisfaction in his announcement.

Sensing that Mr. Petty took some pleasure in this apparent blow to his wife, Amanda asked, "How would you describe your family relationships?"

"Normal." Petty sounded defensive. "We had our differences ... I mean, life doesn't always turn out the way one expects."

"I understand you are a Baptist minister. Was your son involved with the church?"

"Never." Petty did not seem disturbed by this. "Bryce made his own choices."

Amanda wondered if this was a roundabout way

of alluding to Bryce Petty's sexuality. "Tell me about him," she invited.

Petty cleared his throat. "He was a likeable boy. He had a way about him... personable, I suppose you'd call it. He was like me in many ways."

"What kind of work was he in?"

Petty hesitated. "He had his own business for a while, but that didn't work out..."

"What kind of business?"

"Something to do with movies."

"And after that?"

Petty's gaze darted about the room, fixing on the camera. Heavily flushed, he plucked at his tie and rearranged the strands of hair disguising his bald patch. "I have some papers for you, Inspector," he finally said. "If I could have my briefcase."

Austin Shaw stood. "It's at the desk. I'll get it."

"Would you like to take a break, Mr. Petty?" Amanda offered. The guy looked like heart attack material, she thought with a twinge of unease. The last thing she felt like today was having a subject drop dead on her during questioning.

Petty declined. "May as well get it over with."

"When are you going back to Australia?" Amanda asked.

"I'm changing my booking. Have to make arrangements for the body." He paused as Austin Shaw returned with the briefcase, then said, "Guess you don't see the Australian newspapers over here?"

"I pick up *The Age* occasionally," Shaw commented. "Mostly the Saturday edition with the arts supplement."

Petty extracted a bulging envelope from his briefcase and shook out the contents, a pile of newspaper clippings. "You won't have seen these reports, then." He lifted a few at random, reading the headlines, " 'Minister's Son Implicated' . . . 'Spectrum Creditors Meet' . . . 'Sex, Lies and TV' . . ."

Amanda skimmed the information they contained. Spectrum Television, a gay and lesbian broadcaster, had collapsed after losing a defamation suit for half a million dollars in damages. Bryce Petty was president at the time and was named in the lawsuit.

"He disappeared," Petty said, his heavy breathing filling Amanda with alarm.

Exchanging an unhappy look with Austin Shaw, she said, "Perhaps we should continue this later. It's obvious you're distressed, Mr. Petty —"

"No!" He slammed his fist down on the table. "We'll do this now. I'm not coming back here." Grabbing more papers from his briefcase, he thrust them at Amanda. "Look at these."

Conscious of her own pulse accelerating, Amanda stared down at what appeared to be a mortgage document.

"That's our home." Petty said. "We were freehold. I borrowed two hundred and fifty thousand dollars to bail him out of this."

"So you paid the courts?"

Petty was almost purple. "No. Like a fool I gave the money to my son. He disappeared a few days later."

"I see." Amanda poured some water into a tumbler and handed it to Petty. He was hyperventilating, his hands leaving wet smudges on the dark tabletop. Trying to calm him, she said. "I'll order a car for you, Mr. Petty. I think you should have some rest at your hotel. We can resume later in the day —"

Petty didn't seem to hear her. "Have you any idea what this means for me? All over the newspapers. I'll never be able to look anyone in the face again."

Amanda met his eyes. "Was your son insured, Mr. Petty?"

Petty leaped to conclusions. "What are you suggesting? What kind of man do you think I am?"

"Was he?"

"I believe so," Petty glared fixedly at Amanda. "Are you trying to imply I killed my own son?"

"Do you have any idea who might have wanted to harm Bryce?" Austin Shaw interjected.

Petty gave defeated shrug. "I can only accept that it must have been God's will."

That's not how the court would see it, Amanda thought, closing the interview. As Petty stood, she cast him in a mental picture — standing over his son, pulling his head back, pumping that extra un- necessary bullet into his throat. Yes, he was capable of it, she decided. In their next interview, she would make him account for every minute of yesterday afternoon.

An hour later Austin Shaw slid a newspaper feature across Amanda's desk. "Take a look."

Spectrum Television's demise was described in dry detail. Supposedly a nonprofit community broadcaster, the company had several thousand paid-up members whose elected representatives sat on a management committee. Bryce Petty had been president for only a few months when Spectrum broadcast a program he'd produced. It contained visual images of a well-known politician which were cut into the story in such a way that it appeared the politician was engaging in a public sexual act at a notorious gay beat. In the lawsuit that followed, it was shown that Petty had not only edited the film but also gone to some lengths, exploiting his power as president, to avoid clearing it through Spectrum's viewing panel prior to broadcast.

According to Australian law, the office-bearers of an incorporated society were personally liable for its debts in the event of bankruptcy. So Petty and Spectrum's vice president, India Niall, were responsible for half a million dollars in damages. Two other office-bearers had evidently resigned soon after Petty was elected president.

"So this Niall woman was landed with a bill for half the damages?" Amanda noted.

"Interesting, isn't it?" Shaw leafed through his notes. "I've done some homework on her. According to Spectrum's liquidators, her house has been put on the market to resolve her part of the debt. Sounds like Spectrum was originally her vision. She was president for the first year, while everything got going, then she resigned. Petty took over, and within a couple of months half the organization had walked out."

"Popular guy. Has Niall been over here?"

Shaw shook his head. "Not according to Immigration."

"What else do we know about this Spectrum outfit?"

"There's the usual garbage about government money being used to promote the homosexual agenda." Shaw leafed through the newspaper clippings Mr. Petty had supplied. "The program that caused the furor was one Petty produced for Spectrum's current affairs show, his last apparently. There was some kind of walkout by the crew before that. Petty was accused of incompetence and they wanted him off the show. In court a couple of them claimed he made the defamatory episode to spite them."

Amanda twirled her biro between her fingers. "I can't imagine a president destroying his entire organization over some ego problem." It sounded more like the kind of lunatic behavior associated with messy domestic situations . . . men who burned down the family home or killed their own children to punish an ex-wife for rejecting them. "Maybe the guy was just your average idiot," she said. "Made a stupid mistake and couldn't face up to the consequences."

"Maybe someone thought he should," Shaw suggested.

"Moira says he could have died as late as four-thirty."

"Which leaves us precisely nowhere. Awatere's the only person we can place at the scene so far, but his story stacks up."

"That woman on the answer machine . . ."

"The language lab listened to the tape this morning," Shaw said. "It's an Australian accent. The *it's* sounds like *eats*."

"Petty's sister?"

"She's a school teacher in Tauranga. Watertight alibi for yesterday afternoon and she denies making the call. She's flying down here tomorrow morning with her mother."

Amanda frowned. "Mrs. Petty was out here?"

"She came with her husband."

"He wasn't in any hurry to tell us that," Amanda remarked.

"I gather he sent her off to Tauranga to stay with their daughter the day after they got here."

"When did he tell you this?"

"He didn't. It was on the hotel records. He confirmed it when I contacted him."

"What do you think of Mr. Petty?"

"He's a live one." Shaw rocked on his heels. "Could have made the call at three-fifteen to set up an alibi."

Contrary to popular belief most murders were not particularly mysterious, Amanda reflected. Find a motive and you found your killer, especially where money was involved. Petty Senior was the obvious suspect. It was easy to imagine him asking his son to return the money, shooting him when he refused, then hunting for bank account information. "There's got to be some way we can link him to the scene," Amanda said. Until they did, they could not obtain a search warrant for his hotel room. "At this rate he'll be back in Melbourne before we can get anything on him."

"Melbourne . . ." Shaw mused. "The theater's terrific."

Amanda gave him a sharp look. "You'll enjoy a trip over, then?"

He shook his head. "Not possible. My mother's having a growth removed tomorrow."

Amanda dropped her pen with a clatter. "Why didn't you tell me?" She raked her fingers through her hair. "When —"

"She started losing weight a few months ago," Shaw stuck his hands in his pockets and paced back and forth. "She refused to see a doctor at first, but there were other changes . . ."

Once you noticed changes, you were in trouble, Amanda thought. Early intervention. That was the key. She groped for something to say. She had only met the elegant Mrs. Shaw once, a gifted violinist with an international career. "How are you coping?"

Shaw stopped pacing. "Frankly, I'm in a state of disbelief. I can't imagine her ill. I forget she's getting older."

"I can take you off the Petty case," Amanda said. "And if you want special leave I'll talk to the chief."

"There's no need. I'm rostered off tomorrow anyway, and we can play it by ear once she's had the operation."

He must be feeling terrible, Amanda thought, noting for the first time the strain around his eyes. No wonder he'd seemed distracted lately. "I wish I could do something."

"You could handle Melbourne," Shaw suggested mildly. "And leave me in charge at this end. Then I could run my own schedule."

Amanda opened her mouth to refuse, then caught her breath. "I'll think about it," she said.

* * * * *

Police Headquarters lay directly across the road from the City Gallery and Civic Square. It was a prime location — the harbor on one side, city shopping on the other, dozens of small cafés within walking distance. At one of these, City Limits, Roseanne was waiting.

"Am I late?" Inhaling the delicious coffee aroma, Amanda dropped her satchel on the floor and occupied a spindly wooden chair opposite her best friend.

"No. I'm early," said Roseanne. "I quit my job."

Amanda lost her grip on the pita bread square she'd promptly picked up. "You're kidding."

"No," Roseanne said tonelessly. "They can go fuck themselves."

It must be bad, Amanda thought. Roseanne was a social worker with the Juvenile Court. Her patience put her in a class with Catholic martyrs and Inland Revenue tax investigators. "Honey, what happened?" she asked.

"Nothing. That's just the point. It was another day, like every other day. This kid committed suicide. His sister is six months pregnant to their father. She's only fourteen. They've been living in a halfway house. No one gives a shit. It's just another day." Roseanne placed a weary hand on Amanda's. "Don't worry. I'm okay."

"You don't sound okay. Look, maybe you shouldn't rush into this. How about taking a vacation?"

"I can't go back there. I just can't."

Amanda tried to think of something supportive to say. "You can't just quit. What are you going to do?"

"Sleep," Roseanne replied. "Paint my house. I

worked out that if I get two flatmates, I can pay the mortgage. I don't need a lot. The only reason I spend money is to console myself for being depressed."

"I thought you loved your work."

"I'm addicted to it," Roseanne said bitterly. "That's why I'm quitting. I don't have a life, I just have a job."

"Lots of people find their identity in their work," Amanda heard herself saying lamely.

"Yes. Depressing isn't it?" Roseanne swirled her pita bread in the bowl of humus they were sharing. "We get up, get dressed, catch the bus, argue all day with people we don't like, work late, go home, go to bed, get up . . . There's got to be something else."

Burn-out. Amanda recognized the symptoms. Roseanne had allowed everything to get out of proportion and she was too exhausted to take a step back and see what was happening. "You need some time out," Amanda said. "How about going up to the cottage for a while? The dogs would love it."

Roseanne smiled. "I'd like that. I could do some work on the place, build that new gate . . ."

"And I could come up and see you — replace some more floorboards." She and Roseanne shared ownership of a decrepit beach cottage at Otaki, an hour north of the city. Fantastic ocean views, balmy weather, pizza delivery in ten minutes. With the summer crowds long gone, it was the perfect spot for Roseanne to get some peace and quiet.

"I'm thirty-two tomorrow." Roseanne sighed. "I don't want to feel like this."

Amanda put all thoughts of medication out of her head. Roseanne would never touch an anti-depressive. She thought aspirin was hard drugs. "About the job," she ventured. "I was thinking. Wouldn't it be better to keep your options open. I'm sure they'd let you take back your resignation." Amanda knew Roseanne's reputation — they'd grovel on their hands and knees.

"We'll see." Roseanne adopted a placating tone Amanda recognized as a smokescreen. "Let's order. The mushroom burritos are good here."

They were silent for much of the meal. Roseanne switched her gaze between the art work on the walls and the traffic whizzing past the windows. "Have you heard from Debby," she inquired as the waiter removed their plates and took dessert orders.

"I got a letter last week," Amanda said. Debby was in Rwanda making a television special on the aftermath of the genocide. Her access to phones was limited, so Amanda wasn't surprised she didn't hear from her more often.

"I can't believe you let her go," Roseanne said.

Amanda spluttered. "As if I could stop her!"

"I'll bet she would have stayed, if you'd asked her to."

"No chance." Amanda shook her head. "She'd go to the Arctic if she thought it would lift her ratings."

"You're angry with her, aren't you?" Roseanne asked.

"No, I'm not. Why should I be? We talked about it."

Roseanne picked up on her defensive note. "Don't tell me you're still doing this open relationship stuff?"

Amanda hurried over her coffee. She wasn't in the mood to analyze her relationship with Debby Daley. "I know what I'm doing," she told Roseanne.

"You've been saying that for months, but every time I mention Debby, you change the subject."

"That's because there's nothing to discuss. I know you love me, Rosy. I know you long to see me wallowing in domestic bliss. But it's just not realistic. Debby and I have an arrangement. It works for us."

Roseanne's expression was wry. "An arrangement," she echoed. "You live in separate cities, you see other people. I can't believe you're happy with that."

Amanda piled whipped cream on her cherry pie.

"I don't know why we're having this conversation," Roseanne muttered. "I should know better. Why don't I just shut up now. Here —" She pushed her untouched mud cake across the table. "Have this as well. I feel sick."

Amanda met her weary gaze with a pang of guilt. "I'm sorry, Rosy. It's a touchy subject."

"I just want you to be happy."

"I'm a jerk sometimes."

"A nice jerk."

Later they walked arm-in-arm across Civic Square, a sea breeze tugging their clothing. Gulls hovered above Capital Discovery Place, the children's science center, seemingly as entranced as the public by the jade pyramid which crowned it.

"I'll call you," Amanda said when they were in sight of Police Headquarters.

Roseanne pecked her on the cheek. "Have a nice day."

Amanda watched her wander back across the flagstones, head drooping. Some friend I am, she thought guiltily.

CHAPTER FIVE

Harrison was lurking outside Amanda's office, unusually eager to see her. "Anya's here with Sara. She's ready to make a statement."

Relieved, Amanda switched her black woolen jacket for the lightweight version she wore in the office. Even if they couldn't score a conviction, at least they'd have some paper to justify their inquiries.

The two young women were in an interview room, Anya sipping tea, Sara staring blankly ahead.

"Sara," Amanda greeted her warmly. "I'm glad you're here."

Sara turned with painful slowness, as though moving a single muscle was a chore. "Can I speak to you alone?"

"Of course you can." Amanda exchanged a glance with Harrison. Sensing Sara's discomfort with the surroundings, she offered, "Would you like to come up to my office?"

Sara's eyes flickered interest. "Yes, please."

It wasn't ideal, Amanda reflected, as she led the young woman to the elevators. She would have to use her portable tape recorder and the interview would lose value without a second officer present. But it was a beginning. Hopefully Harrison would obtain a useful corroborating statement from Anya. It was looking more like a case by the minute.

Showing Sara into her office, she dragged a couple of chairs into an informal arrangement in front of her desk. "I can even make us some decent coffee," she said as Sara gazed around.

"Did you get these for solving crimes?" Sara pointed at Amanda's citations.

"Most of them are for passing courses. I keep them up there to impress reporters."

With a faint smile, Sara sat down and folded her hands neatly in her lap. "Thank you for looking after me yesterday. I've been feeling pretty bad."

How bad Amanda could only imagine. She drew the curtains, cutting the glare from her tall windows. The fog had lifted temporarily and the harbor glistened sapphire blue in the morning sun.

"It's a nice view," Sara said.

"I got lucky. Most of the offices overlook the city."

"I used to live by the sea. In Napier. That's where I grew up."

Amanda recalled reading something about the small East Coast city which was destroyed by an earthquake back in the thirties. "I've never been there," she said.

"Lots of people visit for the architecture. It's all Art Deco. They built it after the earthquake." Anger registered briefly in Sara's eyes. "I hate the place. I'm never going back."

Roseanne, Amanda thought. The perfect person to help Sara process her feelings. The Accident Compensation Commission paid the therapy costs of sexual violence survivors. Roseanne could earn some income, and Sara would have the best therapy in town. Telling herself to concentrate on the investigation first, Amanda said, "I want to help you, Sara. Will you trust me?"

Sara met her eyes. "I'm here, aren't I?"

Amanda produced her tape recorder and logged the interview. "Is it okay if I record while we talk?"

"I don't know." Sara shifted in her seat. "Who's going to hear it?"

"It's just for our records."

"What's going to happen?" Sara asked.

"What do you want to happen?"

Sara gazed out the window. "I'd like to kill them both."

"There were two people?" Amanda looked longingly at the record button.

"Turn it on." Sara visibly braced herself. "Yes, there were two people. Mel Carter and Jolene Ruth."

"A man and a woman?"

Sara returned her attention to the view, as though willing mind and body elsewhere. "No. They're both women. Mel is short for Melanie."

Amanda felt winded. Two women? It hardly seemed possible. After twelve years on the job, she thought she'd seen it all. Yet not once had she convicted a woman of rape. Accessory, yes. But never rape. "You know these women?"

"I met Mel at a party. She used to be lovers with Jolene."

"Sara. I'm sorry, I know this is difficult, but I have to ask . . ." Amanda felt queasy, her mind returning to the shocking image of the young woman's body during Dr. Rosenberg's examination. "Can you describe exactly what happened?"

Sara's blue eyes swung to Amanda's face. "Is that brandy over there on your shelf?"

Amanda got up and poured a double. I don't want to hear this, she thought, handing Sara the drink. "Sara, you allege you were sexually violated by two women, Melanie Carter and Jolene Ruth, in your flat at three twenty-one Aro Street. Did you see both women clearly?"

"Yes. They didn't blindfold me straightaway."

"How did they gain entry to your flat?"

"I let them in," Sara said bitterly. "I was an idiot. This is all my fault . . ."

"Sara —" Amanda began, but the young woman cut her off.

"I met Mel at a party. Everyone there was so

cool. I felt really stupid ... like I didn't know anything. She was talking about fantasies." She gulped her brandy. "I said I had this fantasy about being tied up and ... and ..."

Amanda could almost see the jurors' faces.

"It was stupid," Sara whispered. "I forgot all about it, then I saw her at Caspers a couple of weeks back and she made these weird comments."

"Like what?"

"I can't remember exactly. She said she had plans for me ... and if I got lucky maybe she'd drop in some time. There was other stuff ... showing off. I think she was drunk "

"Did you invite her home?"

"No," Sara said sharply. "I knew she was only making fun of me."

"Did you see her again after that night?"

"No. Not until it happened."

"You let her into your flat?" Amanda prompted.

"When I opened the door, she slapped my face. Not really hard. But I got a shock and she just kind of walked in ... She said something ... 'Hello, bitch. I'm here to make your dreams come true.' "

"What time was this?"

"About five o'clock."

"What then?"

"She pushed me backwards along the hallway. I tripped on the rug. Then I saw Jolene."

"Where were you?"

"Just outside the lounge door."

"And then ..."

Sara wrapped her arms tightly about herself. "I

thought it was some kind of joke. I tried to get up, but they grabbed me."

"You were forced back down on the floor?"

Sara's eyes were full of self-blame. "I should have fought more. But I started laughing."

Amanda could imagine how a defense attorney would use that information. "Why did you laugh?"

"I suppose I thought it was a game. My dad used to wrestle with us when we were kids. It was kind of like that. I wanted them to stop, but I kept on laughing."

"Did you ask them to stop?"

Her eyes pleaded for belief. "Not then. Later."

"Can you remember what you said, Sara? This is really important," she added, as the young woman retreated into distressed silence. "We have to know whether you consented to anything that happened."

"At first I didn't tell them to stop," she said. "Then when they started to hurt me, I said no. I said it again and again. I think that's why they gagged me in the end. To make me shut up."

"Do you know what time they left your house?"

"I'm not sure. It must have been about seven o'clock. Anya says it was eight when she got home."

Amanda reflected for a moment on how to approach the case. To prosecute successfully they would need an exhaustive account of what had happened. It would be harrowing in the extreme for Sara. "I don't want to put you through this twice, Sara," she said. "If we go down to the interview room now I can get your statement on video and you may not have to appear in court."

"In court?"

"Melanie and Jolene will face charges for what they've done."

Sara lifted her hands to her face in a gesture of dismay. "Oh, God. Will they go to prison?"

"If they're found guilty."

"No one will ever speak to me again."

"Sara," Amanda said gently. "It's not you who committed the crime."

"You don't understand." She lurched to her feet, folding her arms tightly about her waist. "It's such a small community. I have to think . . . I can't talk anymore today."

"It's up to you, Sara." Trying not to reveal her frustration, Amanda concluded the interview. "We can meet again tomorrow."

Sara sought her gaze. "It's just, I don't have anyone else."

"I understand." Amanda escorted her out of the office and down to the interview rooms. Leaving her with Anya, she took Harrison aside. "We need addresses for these individuals," she said, handing over a slip of paper with the names Sara had given her.

Harrison gave the note a brief glance and pushed it into a pocket. "How did it go?"

"Speed wobbles. But we've got enough to work with. As soon as you've tracked down those names, I want you back on the Petty case." Ignoring Harrison's yelp of protest, she said. "You've got a personal stake in this one, so you're off the case."

Harrison took refuge in martyred silence.

Wise move, Amanda thought. A score on the Petty homicide would do much more for her promotion prospects than an unprosecuted rape.

CHAPTER SIX

"Where to, ma'am?" inquired Detective Sergeant Steve Gibbs, a rule-book detective with a solid track record in nailing down rape convictions.

Gibbs had been working out of Auckland CIB until his wife landed a promotion in Wellington late last year. Strictly speaking, Amanda should have handed the case over to the rape squad, but she was aware that Gibbs had career aspirations and fancied his chances of a transfer to homicide. Seconding him onto this case was one way to avoid handing it over.

At the same time she could find out if she wanted him on her team.

He seemed a straight-up kind of guy. Square jaw, white teeth, strong shoulders. A ragged scar tore at the left side of his mouth, etching a knotty path to his ear. "I figured we'd start with Jolene Ruth," Amanda said. "Sounds like she was the accessory and Carter initiated."

It made sense to approach the weaker half of a double act first. They were generally quick to disclaim responsibility and many would finger their partner if they thought it would help their own cause.

Gibbs guided their car out of the underground parking lot and pulled into the early evening traffic congesting Harris Street. Ahead, fog once again blanketed the waterfront, creating a macabre shadow theater of pedestrians and cyclists.

"It's a Mount Victoria address," Amanda said. "Brougham Street."

Gibbs glanced sideways. "Nabbed one there a while back, didn't you?"

"The Crossways rapist," Amanda said. "Used to hang out near the community center and trail women up Brougham."

"Nine lousy years," Gibbs reflected. "What does it take, eh?"

Amanda was silent. In New Zealand the maximum penalty for rape was twenty years. On the rare occasions a judge had awarded the full term, it had been reduced on appeal. Amanda wondered uneasily how a lesbian offender would fare. Badly, if overseas examples were any indication.

Jolene Ruth lived in a renovated Victorian house in expensive Mount Victoria. The door was answered by a woman dressed in striped baggy overalls and a misshapen cardigan. High on her head a mop of poodle-like curls protruded from an African-style headscarf. No doubt the look was trendy in some quarters, but it looked strangely incongruous on a white girl in this remote part of the world, Amanda thought. At the sight of their identification, the woman exhibited the guilty paranoia of someone who had a rolled joint hidden in her trinket box. Her name was Merryn, she said. She was a flatmate of Jolene's. Jolene was sick in bed. She couldn't ask the officers in. They had guests, so it wasn't really appropriate. Hadn't the weather deteriorated after the lovely sunny morning they'd had?

Amanda expressed polite interest in Jolene's illness. "Nothing serious, I hope."

"Just flu," Merryn said. "Everyone's had it."

"Is she off work?"

Merryn vagued out. "Um . . . I'm not sure. I haven't been here for a few days."

"You work in town?"

"I'm a student."

Eternally, Amanda figured.

Merryn glanced behind her once more. "I'll let her know you're here. Excuse me a moment." She closed the door.

Gibbs stuck his hands in his pockets, jiggling a set of keys. "Stalling while they flush their dope down the loo," he muttered.

Amanda caught a whiff of some garlicky cooking fumes. Her breath clouded into damp haze before her.

This was one of those times when all she wanted to do was kick down a door and yell *Police!*

Before she could succumb to temptation, the door was opened by a slender blond woman with a cupid's bow mouth and an expression that coupled innocence and mischief. "Hi. I'm Jolene," she said. There was no need to add *and I'm gorgeous,* but Amanda had the impression she had seriously considered it. Jolene examined their IDs, declaring with bland panache, "I've seen you in the papers, Inspector . . . most impressive. What can I do for you?"

"We're inquiring into a rape that occurred yesterday. I'd like you to look at this photograph and tell me if you recognize this person." Amanda displayed a photograph Sara had provided.

Jolene's gaze strayed to the mufti car parked at the curb, then returned to the photograph. "That's Sara Hart."

"You know Sara?"

"We're acquainted." Jolene blinked rapidly.

"We have reason to believe you can help us with our inquiries," Gibbs said. "Can we talk inside?"

Jolene looked bemused. "I'm having a dinner party."

Entertaining from her sickbed, no doubt. "Then you'd better excuse yourself to your guests," Amanda said, "and we'll take a ride downtown."

Jolene's delicate features froze. "Is that absolutely necessary?"

"Put it this way, Ms. Ruth," Gibbs explained in police idiotspeak. "You can accompany us downtown under caution, or we can arrest you right now on suspicion and you can spend the rest of the night sharing a cell with the kind of people you wouldn't choose to eat dinner with, and we'll interview you when we get 'round to it."

Jolene's face was as pale as her hair, contrasting sharply with a red mark at the base of her throat. Partially obscured by her sweatshirt, it appeared to be a deep scratch. "Naturally I want to assist any way I can." Her tone suggested quite the opposite, but Jolene was obviously weighing up her options. "Please give me a moment to change into something warmer."

Amanda and Gibbs sat out the delay in the car. After fifteen minutes, Gibbs commented, "What do you suppose is keeping her?"

"If she has something to be worried about, she's probably phoning her lawyer."

Gibbs reacted to this like a sniffer dog catching a scent. "How do you want to play this one?"

"I have a feeling Ms. Ruth will try and bring the game to us."

Jolene emerged having exchanged her sweats for a waspish look with vicar's daughter overtones — navy boucle skirt, cream cashmere polo-neck and navy pumps. She appeared to have undergone an attitude transplant as well, her former arrogance supplanted by a fluttering respect. They drove in silence to the station, where, installed in an interview room, she politely requested a cup of tea, checked her watch and murmured abjectly, "I'm so sorry to hold you up, but I can't really say anything until my lawyer gets here."

"His name?" Amanda asked.

"Philip Dyer."

Amanda prevented herself from gasping. Philip

Dyer was one of the hottest defense attorneys in the country, a man who didn't bother to lift the phone for any client worth less than seven figures, unless the case was certain to enhance his media stardom.

Amanda cleared her throat. "I know Mr. Dyer. He's a very busy man, so I suggest we get the formalities out of the way before he arrives."

"The formalities?"

"Your name and date-of-birth details."

Jolene shrugged and offered her passport. According to this, her full name was Jolene Ruth Easton. "I've assumed Ruth as my surname," she explained.

"Why the change?" Amanda asked.

"Is that relevant?"

"Are you related to George Easton?"

The answer was evident in Jolene's studied silence. George Easton was a property speculator, the youngest son of a family already enormously wealthy, thanks to huge timber interests. George had made a second fortune during the rising real estate market of the eighties and had bailed out just before values crashed, leaving thousands of his investors in the lurch.

Presumably Jolene had found it socially expedient to ditch the family name, but she had no intention of rejecting the privilege it conferred. "George Easton is my father," she said with a world-weary air. "But we're not talking right now."

"Have you told Mr. Dyer that?" Amanda asked silkily.

Jolene shrugged. "Philip is a family friend." She glanced around at the sound of a knock.

Barely allowing time for the sergeant to announce

him, Philip Dyer stalked into the interview room, his piercing blue eyes darting from left to right. Dumping his briefcase on the table, he demanded a private consultation with his client. "I assume you have no monitoring equipment switched on, Inspector."

"Only the security cameras."

Satisfied, Dyer assumed his seat opposite a relieved-looking Jolene, lightly patted his lustrous blond hair and extracted a sheaf of papers. As Amanda exited, he called, "Would you mind sending in some coffee, Inspector. Black with sugar."

"That," Amanda informed Gibbs, "is what Moira McDougall calls the mother of all snags."

"Dyer, a sensitive New Age guy?" Gibbs was clearly unconvinced.

Amanda smiled wryly. "No. You lose your fly, your line, your thousand-dollar rod and reel, and the goddamn fish too, unless you're very careful."

While they were absent, Dyer had obviously briefed his client. He had also set up his own recording equipment, just to ensure the police tapes showed no evidence of tampering in the unlikely event the case came to trial.

After reading Jolene her rights once more for Dyer's benefit, Amanda said. "I understand you wish to make a statement. Have you prepared something?"

Dyer raised his coiffed head from a pile of scribbled sheets. "My client desires to cooperate fully with police inquiries, Inspector. She is prepared to answer your questions before submitting any additional statement."

"Very well." Amanda focused on Jolene. "Ms. Ruth —"

"Jolene is fine," said Jolene.

Amanda pushed the photograph of Sara across the table. "Can you identify this woman?"

"It's Sara Hart."

"What is your relationship to Sara?"

"I'm informally acquainted with her."

"How long have you known her?"

"We first met four weeks ago."

"Could you describe the circumstances of that meeting?"

"A friend of mine introduced her. We were at a party."

"Your friend's name?"

"Mel . . . Melanie Carter."

"How did Melanie Carter know Sara?"

Jolene glanced at Dyer, who gave the briefest of nods. "She met her at the gym."

"What is the nature of their relationship?"

Again a nod from Dyer. "It was sexual."

"What is your relationship to Mel?"

Jolene's head drooped. Amanda couldn't hear her reply.

Dyer supplied a dry answer. "My client was involved in a sexual liaison with Melanie Carter at one time. They are now on distant terms."

"Jolene, is that an accurate description of your relationship with Mel?" Amanda asked.

Jolene met her eyes, then quickly looked away. "I guess so," she said flatly. "Yes."

"When did you last see Sara Hart?"

Jolene's hands were trembling. She transferred them from the tabletop to her lap. "Five o'clock last night," She coughed, then sipped some water, her hands suddenly shaking. "It all went wrong. We —"

"My client is unwell," Dyer swiftly interjected.

Read, inadmissible statement. Just as swiftly Amanda asked, "Are you on any medication, Jolene?"

"No —" Jolene glanced at Dyer, then fell silent.

Amanda poured some water into a glass and took her time about drinking it. "What were you doing at Sara's place last night?"

"We watched a video and had a few drinks," Jolene said.

"Who was present?"

"There was just me, Sara and Mel. Sara's flatmate was at work."

"How do you know that?"

"Mel told me."

"Sara was physically assaulted and sexually violated in the course of the evening," Amanda said. "Tell me about that."

Unmoved by his client's pleading gaze, Dyer instructed, "Tell the Inspector exactly what you told me, Jolene."

"Sara and Mel were acting up," Jolene said.

Amanda raised her eyebrows.

"Playing around!" Jolene's eyes glittered with brief bright anger. "Sex games."

"In your presence?"

"That was the general idea." She made a futile attempt to sound blasé. "Mel had set up some kind of fantasy scene with Sara. She wanted me to go along. Just to watch. It was part of the fantasy."

Amanda gave her an old-fashioned look. "How long have you known Mel?"

Jolene ran a hand across her damp forehead. "Two years."

"Do you consider her to be a violent person?"

Dyer chipped in. "Jolene, explain to the Inspector what you know about Mel Carter's lifestyle."

Jolene looked twitchy. "Recently she's been getting into leather. Nothing serious . . . more of a fashion thing really. Then she got the hots for Sara." Her voice grew bitter. "I mean, Sara was a virgin and everything and she was really impressed with Mel."

It got worse by the minute. The media would eat it up, Amanda thought. As if there weren't enough negative stereotypes of lesbians already.

"Mel's not normally violent, but if she's been drinking . . ."

"Was she drinking alcohol at Sara's?"

"I think she had some beer."

"Did you drink?"

"Yes."

"Would you say you were drunk?"

At this point Dyer, who had been scribbling constantly, silenced Jolene. "Let's not get carried away," he said mildly. "My client is exhausted. She has given me a statement about the events of yesterday evening." He handed Amanda a neatly written summary. "If you have any other questions we could arrange a time for tomorrow."

Amanda read the statement. Jolene described how Mel had seized Sara and tied her hands. At first Sara had giggled and played along. She became less co-operative when Mel slapped her and told her to shut up. Jolene had felt uncertain, but Mel assured her that this was a fantasy being acted out and she had

71

discussed it with Sara ahead of time. Mel made threats to Sara, slapping her face. Mel was also drinking alcohol. Upset and scared, Jolene said she would leave unless Mel let Sara go. Mel accused her of being jealous. Shortly afterward, Jolene left.

"Have you read this account, Jolene?" Amanda asked.

Jolene nodded. "It's all there."

"If you were so upset by what was going on why didn't you call the police?"

Jolene took a long time to answer. "Because it was between Mel and Sara."

"I see." Amanda stood. "If you'll excuse me for a moment, I'll get this typed." Suspending the interview she left the room and signaled Gibbs to accompany her.

Outside the door, Gibbs scanned the statement. "Stitching her buddy up nicely."

"And setting herself up as a Crown witness, if I read Dyer correctly," Amanda said.

Gibbs read the statement again. "You buy it?"

"Not for a minute."

"She claims she left before this Mel character."

"Not according to Sara." Amanda had also picked up the discrepancy.

"But Sara was blindfolded, wasn't she?" Gibbs noted the point any defense attorney would make. "Let me have a crack at her," he said, opening the door.

"Be my guest." With an curt nod to Dyer, Amanda said, "Before we get this typed out, Detective Sergeant Gibbs has a few more questions for Jolene."

Gibbs took Amanda's place, leaning back in the

chair, legs outstretched, his body language that of a man who knew much more than he was letting on. "What time did you leave Sara Hart's apartment last night, Jolene?" he asked softly.

"About six," Jolene said.

"After you'd watched videos, consumed some beer and tied up young Sara. Action-packed hour." Gibbs unfurled some gum and popped it into his mouth, chewing reflectively. "What made you leave so soon?"

"I was upset"

"About your friend Mel and Sara? What were they doing exactly?"

Jolene fidgeted. "They were having sex."

"Can you be more specific?" Gibbs chewed placidly.

"Christ, what else do you want to know!" Jolene ran shaking fingers through her hair. "I was supposed to watch them doing it, but I couldn't. So I went."

"At six?"

Jolene glanced tensely at Dyer. "More or less. Maybe it was a little later. I'm not sure."

"Which door did you leave by?"

"The front."

"You were alone?"

Jolene sighed. "I left them to it. I'd had enough."

"Of watching?" Gibbs uncrossed his legs and leaned forward, elbows on the table. "Is that why your friend Mel invited you along? She knows you like that sort of thing. Watching?"

Dyer snapped his briefcase shut. "That's enough, Detective. My client has admitted she was foolish and she's willing to assist you any way she can —"

73

"Then she can answer my questions," Gibbs said. "When did Melanie Carter invite you along on this . . . er . . . fantasy, Ms. Ruth?"

"A few days ago. Sunday, I think."

"You planned it together?"

"No! She and Sara planned it. She asked me to come because they needed someone else there."

"To watch?"

"For heaven's sake. I've told you this," Jolene snapped.

"But you didn't enjoy watching, did you?" Gibbs paused. "I'm confused, Jolene. If you don't like watching, why did you go along? It doesn't make any sense, does it? Did you expect to be taking a different role?"

"No!" Jolene compressed her lips.

"You went along to participate, didn't you?" Gibbs dropped his voice. "That's how you come by that scratch on your neck."

Dyer stood. "You can speculate as much as you wish, Detective. But my client has given you a statement of events and that is all she has to say, at this stage."

"Your client is lying," Amanda said.

Dyer oozed confidence. "I think a jury would find my client very convincing."

"Especially when they know where she works," Amanda stared pointedly at Jolene. "Are you full time at the Rape Crisis Center, Jolene, or just part time?"

Jolene stared at the tabletop and mumbled something indistinct. Even Dyer's composure ruptured for a split second.

Exchanging a look with Gibbs, Amanda continued, "As an experienced rape crisis worker, I'm interested to know your opinion on whether Sara was raped by Mel."

Jolene stared into an empty corner of the room. "It's not that simple."

"Really?" Amanda leafed through her notes. "Sara says she was crying and saying no and Mel proceeded to penetrate her with fingers and objects."

"That must have happened after I'd gone." Jolene said.

"But you've already said they were having sex when you left," Gibbs said. "What exactly do you mean by that?"

"I couldn't see what Mel was doing," Jolene said tonelessly.

"What about Sara?"

Jolene swallowed and did not reply.

"Tell me, Jolene. Did you at any stage hear Sara ask Mel to stop what she was doing?"

With a silencing glance at Jolene, Dyer said, "My client will sign a record of this interview. I presume she is free to go now."

"Please answer my question, Jolene," Amanda persisted. "Did you hear Sara say no?"

Avoiding her gaze, Jolene stood.

"You're in a shitload of trouble —" Amanda began.

"Don't try and intimidate my client, Inspector," Dyer said. "This interview is over." Impatiently he responded to the feeble bleep of his mobile phone, excusing himself to take the call outside the interview room.

Staring after him Jolene sagged back down in her chair. After a moment's silence, she said softly, "I suppose you're going to arrest her now."

Amanda met her eyes. "Are you saying a crime was committed?"

Jolene cradled her head in her hands. "Someone bring me a Diet Coke."

CHAPTER SEVEN

Melanie Carter was out of town, according to the bar staff at Caspers. Sure, they knew her. She broke a couple of their pool cues in a competition two weeks ago and still hadn't paid for them. They hadn't seen her lately and yes, they recognized Sara from the photo. Nice kid, one of them said.

"Time for an arrest warrant," Gibbs said as they returned to the car.

"Let me know when you've got her," Amanda said. "I need to get back on the Petty homicide."

"How's it looking?"

"More and more like a professional hit." She gave a sharp humorless laugh. "Not really. I'm sure the guy was done by someone who knew him. Unfortunately most of our leads are across the Tasman."

"Free trip for some lucky bastard," Gibbs remarked. "You'll be killed in the rush."

"I may have to go myself."

"Brave sacrifice."

They turned into Courtenay Place hunting for a parking space. The smell of Chinese food hit them as soon as they got out of the car.

"Pork buns," Gibbs remarked. "My wife says that red dye is poisonous."

They walked briskly toward the Tong Shun, passing the Paramount Cinema where a bunch of art-house types were lined up for a Krzysztof Kieslowski rerun.

"Seen it?" Gibbs asked.

Amanda shook her head. The last time she'd been to the movies was months ago when Debby had scored free tickets to a mindless action thriller. All Amanda could remember was a car chase and protracted shots of the musclebound star. *The director must be in love with him,* she had muttered after a particularly laughable sequence. *He is the director,* Debby said.

"My wife reckons we don't get out enough," Gibbs remarked. "She says I'm married to the job. She can talk."

"She's a doctor, isn't she?"

"Yeah. Burns specialist. Skin grafts. She's been researching this new artificial skin stuff. It's a real big deal —" He broke off, as if embarrassed to be caught bragging about his wife's achievements.

They studied the take-out menu on the restaurant wall.

"We usually go for a double combination rice, a couple of *bami goreng,* a sweet and sour and the banquet assortment," Amanda said.

"Sounds good to me." Gibbs opened the refrigerator and selected an assortment of sodas.

"You want extra pork buns?" Amanda asked.

Gibbs grinned, the scarred side of his face contorting. "Yeah. I like to live on a knife's edge."

Austin Shaw had spent three hours interviewing Jim Petty, he said, yawning.

"And?" Amanda chewed a mouthful of noodles.

"Bryce Petty didn't leave a will, so Mom and Dad get everything."

"It's mostly theirs anyway, isn't it?"

"His life insurance is worth five hundred grand."

Amanda whistled. "You think his father did it?"

"With that kind of money coming he could have paid someone else to get their hands dirty," Shaw said.

"We should be so lucky."

New Zealand was a small country where most of the population had never seen a gun, much less owned one. It was almost impossible for a professional criminal to keep a low profile, so paid hits were typically carried out by desperate junkies or small-time criminals looking for the big time. None of them could keep their mouths shut. Typically they got themselves noticed by flashing the proceeds around.

"The old man's definitely covering something up," Shaw said.

"How does his alibi check out?"

"He was seen in his hotel room at two-thirty by a bellboy delivering some dry cleaning. Between three-thirty and four-thirty he says he was in a meeting with the Bishop of Wellington. Then he went to the museum. We've requested security camera footage and I'll be taking a statement from the bishop later today."

Amanda sipped her Coke gloomily. "And Mrs. Petty was out of town . . . very convenient."

"I've told Mr. Petty we need to speak to her and the sister," Shaw said. "He didn't welcome the idea."

"Did he tell you Bryce was gay?"

"He didn't need to," Shaw commented with dry humor. "Since when did straight men buy their condoms in bulk?"

The remark said nothing about Shaw, Amanda decided. Simple detection would lead anyone to the same conclusion. "How's your mom?" she asked.

"I took her to the hospital after I finished with Petty. They're operating in the morning." Shaw wiped his mouth with a paper napkin. "She seems resolved."

Amanda was conscious of how little she knew of Austin Shaw. She could only guess what he must be feeling, an only child with no living relatives apart from his mother. His father had left them before Austin could walk. "If there's anything I can do . . ." she offered.

Shaw scraped the rest of his meal into the trash. "Thanks."

Amanda drove home via Melanie Carter's address in Mount Cook. The ground floor of a decrepit wooden semi-detached, the place was in darkness, not even a porch light on. Amanda squeezed a few fingers into the letterbox. Either Mel didn't get much mail or someone had been clearing it. The front door rattled when she knocked. There was no response. Loosening the flap on her shoulder holster, she peered into the gaps between the curtains. Nothing moved.

A narrow brick pathway led around the back of the house into an overgrown courtyard. The place smelled of dead things — moldy leaves, rotten wood, unpicked fruit decaying on trees. Knee deep in weeds, Amanda shone her torch around. A few socks dangled limply from the clothesline, cobwebs between them. Boxes of empty beer and wine bottles were stacked against the corrugated iron fence next to an incinerator that had rusted through. Amanda poked through the sodden ashes with a stick. Behind her something moved and her hand went automatically to her gun. "Police," she said, turning sharply.

There was nothing. Just the earth's lisping protests as it absorbed the relentless moisture of winter, the deadly hum of power lines overhead. Conscious of a faint flash of white on the periphery, Amanda directed her beam at the mountain of empty bottles. A pair of luminous round eyes blinked at her and a cat sprang down, vanishing into the weeds.

Amanda felt her shoulders sag with relief. A moment later the cat rubbed across her legs. Surprised, she stooped to stroke it. Not fully grown, its body was skeletal, fur harsh, belly bulging unnaturally. "Poor baby," she murmured. "You're starving."

The cat responded to her sympathetic tone with a tragic meow. It seemed accustomed to human touch, not timid as a wild cat might be. Perhaps it was someone's lost pet. Cautiously Amanda lifted it into her arms. "Let's take a ride," she said.

"I don't believe this," Roseanne laughed into the phone. "You found a stray cat and took it home?"

"She's still eating," Amanda said.

"Don't let her have too much at once. She'll only throw up all over your new carpet."

Heeding this advice, Amanda refrained from spooning more sardines into the bowl. "You should see her face. It's long and narrow like a Siamese, and she has these amazing green eyes."

"And she's black?"

"With a white tuft on the tip of her tail."

"When are you taking her to the SPCA?"

"Er . . ."

"You already have a cat," Roseanne reminded her.

"I think Madam's lonely."

Silence.

"She's been kind of neurotic ever since I came back," Amanda said.

"You were away a year. It's a long time for a cat."

"I think she misses your dogs." Roseanne had looked after Madam while Amanda spent a year back home in New York, trying to figure out whether she wanted to return there permanently.

"She hated the dogs," Roseanne said. "She ate a piece of Rupert's ear. It was not passion."

"Her stomach sticks out a lot." Amanda surveyed the scrawny black cat, now washing herself beside the refrigerator as if she owned it. "Do you think it's worms."

"Definitely. Give her two of those tablets Debby left on the top shelf of the pantry."

"What tablets?"

"Take a look. Debby told me about them."

Balancing the phone against her ear, Amanda opened the pantry and took down a small red packet. Debby had tucked a note inside the box which said, *Don't forget the repeat dose in four weeks.*

"You should get her vaccinated, too," Roseanne said. "It'll save the SPCA doing it."

"Right," Amanda said.

"You are taking her to the SPCA tomorrow, aren't you?"

"Sure."

"Amanda?"

"I'm looking forward to the party," Amanda said feebly.

"Lots of interesting women are coming," Roseanne said. "That actress you fancy — Roberta Craig — I've invited her. And Jessamyn Masters, the lawyer with the gorgeous green eyes."

"I can't wait." Amanda's stomach felt hollow.

They said their good-byes.

Amanda put the phone back on the hook and poured some milk into a bowl. "What am I going to call you?" she asked her feline visitor.

CHAPTER EIGHT

Mrs. Ada Petty was a dumpy woman with permed gray curls and watery blue eyes that protruded slightly behind thick gold-framed glasses. She seemed misplaced in the nineties, her demeanor that of a bedazzled fifties housewife in a quiz show.

"I'm sorry about this," Amanda said as a female constable closed the interview room door and checked the monitoring equipment.

"Don't worry, dear," Mrs. Petty said. "You've got a job to do."

Certain her overbright manner concealed shock

and grief, Amanda said, "Please accept my condolences. We'll do our very best to find the person responsible for this and bring him to justice."

Mrs. Petty clasped her plump hands together and shot a darting glance toward the door. "I don't understand why Jim has to wait out there."

"We've already interviewed Mr. Petty," Amanda explained in a conciliatory tone. "All we need now is a brief statement from you. Tell me, Mrs. Petty, do you drive?"

"Drive?" Mrs. Petty barely seemed to comprehend the question.

"Do you have a driver's license?"

"Yes. It's in my handbag."

"I understand you've been staying with your daughter in Tauranga for a few days," Amanda said. The sooner Mrs. Petty's alibi was confirmed, the sooner the poor woman could be left to grieve in peace. "When did you leave Wellington?"

"On Tuesday. We made an early start. It's a long way."

"Wouldn't it have been easier for your daughter to fly down and see you?"

"Oh, no." Mrs. Petty looked askance. "She has her job. I couldn't ask that of her."

"We've spoken with the people you traveled with," Amanda said. "They mentioned you were carsick and broke your trip in Taupo."

Mrs. Petty nodded. "I stopped overnight at a nice motel near the hot baths."

Amanda took down the name and address. "And you flew to Tauranga the next day?"

"That's right, dear." She adopted a confiding tone. "Just between you and me, I was happy to let my friends drive on without me. They're smokers, you see."

"What time did you arrive in Tauranga on Wednesday?"

"Around six." Her eyes started to water. "Glenys picked me up from the airport. We got the call later that night."

Amanda waited for her to wipe her glasses. "It must have been a terrible shock."

Mrs. Petty nodded mutely.

"Tell me about Bryce," Amanda said.

"He was a lovely little boy, the apple of his father's eye. Jim was just a teeny bit disappointed when Glenys was born. Never said as much, but when Bryce came along...proud as punch. Men!" She attempted to engage Amanda in a conspiratorial smile.

"Were Glenys and Bryce close?"

"Not like some brothers and sisters. It's hard when the girl is older. Glenys never really understood there's some things boys can do that girls can't — certain liberties. You can't tell them it's for their own good, can you?"

"How is Glenys taking the loss?" Amanda asked.

Mrs. Petty looked uncertain, as if suspecting a trick question. "She's been very quiet...what's the word — looking inward..."

"Introspective?"

"Yes. That's Glenys. Always an introspective girl. You're never quite sure what she's thinking."

"Maybe she should have been a detective," Amanda said lightly.

Mrs. Petty seemed nonplussed. "Oh, my goodness! A detective. It's hardly the job for a woman." She flushed. "I'm sure it's different for you, Inspector, being an American and all . . ."

Amanda refrained from making a cynical remark. Mrs. Petty obviously didn't have a feminist bone in her body. She had no doubt reared her daughter to have limited expectations and her son to view the world as his oyster. "Do you have a career yourself, Mrs. Petty?" she asked.

Something flickered across the creaseless passivity of her stare. "I'm a homemaker. My family is my career."

Defensive, Amanda thought. A touchy subject. She prodded a little more. "Did you have a job before you were married?"

Mrs. Petty shook her head. "I was in my third year at University. In those days you didn't work once you got married. And with Jim in the church and the two children, I had my hands full."

"You never completed your degree?"

"It's a shame, really." She sounded resigned. "But I did my duty as a wife and mother. I'm proud of that."

"So there's just you and Mr. Petty now?"

Mrs. Petty cleared her throat. "Bryce came back home for a while when the trouble happened. He was supposed to stay until everything was sorted out."

"When was the last time you saw your son?" Amanda asked softly.

Mrs. Petty plucked at the ball of damp tissue in her hand. "He took us out to dinner the night before he disappeared. It was supposed to be a celebration. Jim had given him the money, you see. He was going to pay off the debt and make a fresh start."

"You had no idea what he was planning?"

Mrs. Petty clasped and unclasped her hands. "He was gone the next day. Just like that. Not even leave a note." Her eyes found Amanda's. "I told Jim, you know. But he wouldn't listen."

"What did you tell your husband?"

"Not to give him the money." Her chest rose and fell with suppressed sobs.

"Why?"

"Because it wasn't fair," she whispered. She seemed about to add something then broke off abruptly, her eyes flooding with tears.

"Fair?" Amanda repeated.

"Temptation," Mrs. Petty said. "Jim should have known better."

Amanda gave her a moment to compose herself, then said, "Do you have any idea who might have killed Bryce?"

Mrs. Petty shook her head. Her expression had become remote. "I suppose we have to go back and arrange the funeral now."

Jim Petty stood as they returned to the waiting room. Placing a proprietorial arm around his wife's shoulders, he demanded, "Are you quite finished, Inspector?"

Amanda nodded. "Constable Taylor will drive you back to the hotel."

"That won't be necessary." He assisted his expressionless wife into her coat. "I think a brisk walk would do us both good."

As they walked over to the elevators, Amanda noticed Mrs. Petty limping slightly. A support bandage swathed her left ankle. The flesh above it was swollen and discolored. The steel doors opened and they entered, turning to face outwards. For a split second Mrs. Petty held Amanda's stare, then she looked sharply away.

"That white Mitsubishi." Harrison pushed tangled copper curls off her forehead. "We've got four sightings now — the neighbor, Mrs. Carsen, and the bloke over the road who was watching Ricki Lake, a couple of schoolkids who were doing a pamphlet run, and a guy walking a dog."

She had pieced together the car's movements, she informed the small group of detectives gathered for the briefing. Shoving miniature blue flags into the enlarged streetmap on the inquiry center wall, she said the Mitsubishi had entered the parking lot at two-thirty and departed at about ten minutes after three, passing the guy walking the dog. The kids doing the pamphlet run saw it at quarter past three when it failed to halt for them at a pedestrian crossing on Tinakori Road. Anticipating the next question, Harrison said, "No one got a decent look at the driver. The guy with the dog thought it was a woman, but the kids thought it was a man. There was no one else in the vehicle."

"Age, hair color?" Amanda asked.

"Sunglasses, dark coat, pale scarf. That's what they all agree on. The kids thought he might have been wearing a hat. They were great, actually. They tried to memorize the registration number. I think they were pretty annoyed the car didn't stop at the crossing." She wrote several combinations on the whiteboard. "If we accept that the letters and first digit are correct, we've got about a thousand cars to check. Narrowed down to Mitsubishis we're looking at two hundred."

Amanda continued the briefing, describing her interview with Mrs. Petty and a fruitless five minutes with Glenys who merely verified that she had picked her mother up from Tauranga Airport at six-thirty on Wednesday.

Detective Sergeant Solomon had nothing on the murder weapon, except a confirmation from ballistics that they were looking for a .38 revolver, probably a Smith & Wesson Model 10. The nitrate tests they'd run on Awatere showed up negative. "Shame Mr. Petty declined the test," he said. "My money's on him."

"We have nothing to place him at the scene," Amanda said. "And his alibi is strong." She glanced at Harrison. "Got anywhere with the deceased's bank?"

Harrison groaned. "You'd think I was planning a robbery. They won't release a thing until they have a Court order and permission from his next of kin. It'll be next Monday, at least."

"The Pettys are out of here tomorrow, right?" Solomon interrupted.

"Unfortunately," Amanda said. "Which brings me to our next problem. Someone has to go to Melbourne. D.S. Shaw is unavailable. Solomon?"

"I'll go," Nikora volunteered.

"You're on a course next week, remember?" Harrison reminded him sharply.

"It's not a problem." Solomon said. "My wife's due to have the baby any day, but her sister will give her a hand."

With the other seven, or was it eight, children?

"Fine," Amanda said. "We'll get you on a flight tomorrow."

Solomon's brow creased. "Tomorrow?"

"Is there a problem?"

"It's my girl. The oldest. Got a big match on. Mixed side."

"Sunday then." Even as she said it, Amanda remembered Solomon, deeply religious, did not work on Sundays. It was in his employment agreement as a special condition.

"She's good, that girl of yours," Nikora enthused. "Big! Man, she'll ice those Marist kids!"

Solomon grinned. "Been training her since she was four. She's into weights now."

Amanda tried to tell herself one rugby game was the same as another. What did it matter if Solomon missed his daughter just this once?

"Two tries away from the fourteen-year-old record." Solomon glowed with anticipation. "First time a girl ever did it. This'll be the match."

"Monday then," Amanda muttered.

"There's no Monday flight to Melbourne," Harrison said. "Just Tuesday."

"This is a homicide investigation," Amanda said irritably. And she was supposed to be leading it, she thought. Shaw's mother was in surgery. Solomon's daughter was about to take a glory run, and his wife was about to give birth again. She glanced at Harrison and immediately rejected the idea of sending the junior detective alone. "Book me on the Sunday flight," she said.

* * * * *

Glenys Petty bore little resemblance to her chunky parents. Tall and fine-boned with silky light brown hair falling loosely about her shoulders, she was not a beauty in the classical sense. But she had a quiet charm about her that seemed English rather than Antipodean.

Amanda had not expected to see her again after their brief interview earlier that morning, but it seemed Glenys had something on her mind. She'd called just before lunch asking Amanda to meet her for coffee at the Lido café.

As usual the place was crowded with people who wanted to be seen. Amanda squeezed her way to a non-smoking table near the concave windows. Glenys was absorbed in some weighty looking reading. She glanced up sharply as Amanda greeted her, then closed her book, marking the page with an embroidered ribbon.

"Is it good?" Amanda glanced at the title. *Wild Swans*. Something to do with China.

Glenys slid the book into her handbag. "It's fascinating. Completely tragic."

"Bestseller, huh?" Amanda sat down. "You wanted to see me . . ."

Glenys nodded. There was a suppressed air about her, as if she lived her life from a distance. During their earlier conversation, she had seemed painfully circumspect, answering Amanda's questions with the careful calculation of a person who had her own theory but did not want to reveal it. Perhaps she'd changed her mind, Amanda thought.

The waitress brought over the espresso Amanda had ordered and Glenys requested another pot of peppermint tea. After a meaningless opening comment about the cold weather, she said, "I want to talk to you about my father. I know you suspect him."

Amanda did not bother to deny it.

"I suspected him too. For about five minutes. Then I knew he couldn't have done it."

"You sound very sure of that."

"You have to understand, my father adored Bryce. It never mattered what he did . . ."

"Including his sexuality?"

Looking her straight in the eye, Glenys said, "My father has been having extramarital affairs with men since I was a child, so he could hardly throw stones at Bryce." Amanda's face must have shown her astonishment, for she added cynically, "The last person you'd suspect, isn't he? I only figured it out myself recently. He and I had a talk . . . one of *those* talks. I'd been in therapy for a year and I confronted him over a few issues. I won't bore you with the details . . ."

"I'll let you know if I'm falling asleep," Amanda said.

Glenys picked a tiny piece of peppermint leaf from her tea. "I spent my whole childhood trying to impress him, but it was a complete waste of time. He was only interested in Bryce. It was all very narcissistic of course. Mom and I merely existed to clean up after them and make them look good. That's one of the reasons I moved here. I just couldn't stand the hypocrisy any longer." She gave a tight little laugh. "Nuclear families . . . wonderful, aren't they?"

"You said you confronted your father . . ."

"We haven't spoken since. I told him exactly what

I thought of him and his son. At least Bryce had the guts to live openly as a gay person. Dad's still using Mom as a human shield." She stared into space for a long moment, then said, as if she were talking to herself, "I'm not going to turn out like her."

"Does your mother know about your father's relationships?" Amanda asked.

"I think she suspects him of seeing other women. But gay?" Glenys shook her head. "No one would believe it."

"How did you find out?"

"Bryce told me. He saw Dad in a sauna."

Amanda caught her breath, struck by an idea. It seemed completely irrational for Petty Senior to have given such a large sum of money directly to his son instead of paying the court. But perhaps there was a simple explanation. The more she thought about it, the more plausible it seemed.

The Spectrum affair had served up a perfect opportunity. Bryce had threatened his father with exposure but promised, in exchange for the money, that he would keep quiet and vanish. His father had paid up, ostensibly a long-suffering parent buying his kid out of trouble. Had he intended all along to cry foul, follow his son, kill him and take the money back, cashing in on the fat insurance policy at the same time? It was possible, Amanda decided. Blackmail and murder often went hand in hand.

Suspecting Glenys Petty was trying not to draw the same conclusion, she asked, "Why do you think your father gave Bryce that money instead of paying it to the courts?"

"Incredible, isn't it. The only thing I can think of is that Dad was trying to prove something. He's quite ill, you see. He had heart surgery last year and now they've found what looks like a brain tumor."

Uncertain what she was getting at, Amanda said, "Then surely he had even more reason to be careful with his money."

"Normally that would be true," Glenys said. "But I think he feels he has nothing to lose. I mean, he's due for retirement anyway, and he may not live to collect his pension for long. This was his chance." Responding to Amanda's puzzlement, she added, "To prove he was right and my mother was wrong."

"In what way?"

"Mom didn't want to lend Bryce the money. She said they'd never get it back. But Dad insisted. He's always kidded himself about Bryce."

"He must have been furious when Bryce disappeared." Even if Glenys was right and Jim Petty had shot himself in the foot in a game of point-scoring with his wife, it was still a motive.

Glenys nibbled half-heartedly on one of the tiny almond biscuits that had accompanied their drinks. "That's the strange thing," she said. "He only got mad when Mom hired the detective."

Amanda put her cup down. In Jim Petty's statement to Austin Shaw, he had claimed the private detective was his idea.

"He wanted her to sack the guy," Glenys continued. "Mom said he made a bunch of excuses for Bryce . . . like he had panicked and he was under too much pressure. It was almost as if he didn't care about the money. He said they'd work something out when Bryce came back."

"But your mother traced him?"

"You know why I think Dad came here," Glenys said bitterly. "To stop Mom. She would have turned Bryce over to the police and Dad couldn't stand that. So he acted like he was angry about the money too, and said he would handle everything. He couldn't get her out of the way fast enough."

Amanda's thoughts returned to the blackmail scenario. What if Jim Petty had intended to pay off his precious son and let him vanish? Then, just when he thought his career and reputation were safe, his wife had tracked Bryce down. Knowing the game would be up if she spoke to Bryce, he got her out of the way, bought a gun, and shut Bryce up for good, getting his money back at the same time. It made complete sense.

"You've been really helpful," she told Glenys. It was sad, she thought. Despite his failings as a parent, Jim Petty's daughter was still trying to protect him.

Perhaps guessing she'd said nothing to persuade Amanda of her father's innocence, Glenys clasped her hands together anxiously, "I don't think I've been clear. What I'm saying is Dad came here to warn Bryce, not kill him. He might have thought he could talk him into giving the money back . . . threaten him with the police, or something."

"And maybe Bryce refused," Amanda said softly. "Killing someone is a very effective way to silence them."

"You don't believe me." Glenys concentrated on Amanda's face, her clear brown eyes pleading. "Look, I have no reason to try and protect my father. I despise him. If he did it, I really hope you catch him. But you could waste a lot of time chasing the wrong person."

"Do you have some idea who the right person is?" Amanda asked.

Glenys averted her eyes. "That tape you played me . . . of the woman who phoned Bryce. My mother said someone came to see her not long after he vanished. She had something to do with the Spectrum business. She was looking for Bryce."

"Your mother didn't mention this to me."

"She probably didn't think it was important. This whole experience has been terrible for Mom. She feels responsible . . . the usual maternal guilt trip. She brought up a son who turned out to be a liar and a thief — where did she go wrong?"

"How did *you* feel about your brother?" Amanda's mind was working overtime. Was there any way Glenys could have pulled that trigger? Was hers the voice on the answer machine? It was definitely similar. She had admitted she knew Bryce's phone number, saying her mother had told her a few days before the Pettys arrived in New Zealand.

"I know what you're thinking," Glenys said. "But believe me, I wouldn't ruin my life over Bryce. I hated him when we were kids. Whenever he did something wrong, he always managed to avoid the consequences. It was incredible. Either he'd lay the blame on me or he'd pull this pathetic misunderstood act and people would feel sorry for him. I think he's the most manipulative person I've ever known."

"I'm surprised he held such an important job with Spectrum," Amanda said.

Glenys shrugged. "I'm not. Bryce is just like

Dad — an expert at making himself look good." She paused reflectively. "If I know my brother, someone else has been paying for his mistakes and got sick of it. That's the person you should be looking for, Inspector. One of my brother's scapegoats."

CHAPTER NINE

Amanda buttoned her jacket then unbuttoned it. The deep wine color teamed well with the gray pin-stripe trousers Debby had chosen for her. In fact the whole outfit looked surprisingly good, especially with her ultra-shiny new black shoes. Amanda gelled her hair and flattened it into a smooth, wet-look style Debby had taught her. Some L'Egoïste perfume, her overcoat, Roseanne's present, bottle of wine, and she was ready.

Dubiously she stared at her bed. Laid out neatly on the quilt were her Smith & Wesson .357, shoulder holster, handcuffs, collapsible riot stick, flashlight, ID and cellular phone. She slid the ID into her pants pocket — don't leave home without it — and picked up the mobile phone. It bulged awkwardly in the jacket, destroying the smooth lines. Irritated at the impracticality of the garment, Amanda donned her overcoat and dropped the phone into a capacious side pocket. She then stuffed everything else into the drawer beneath her bed and locked it.

Perhaps she should have kept the cuffs out, she thought suddenly. Roseanne would be furious. Handcuffs at her birthday party. Amanda stared down at the drawer, then unlocked it and extracted the cuffs. Her eyes were drawn to the .357. No, she told herself. That would really be pushing her luck. Besides, she had a .22 stashed beneath her car seat, just in case.

It was nine o'clock when she arrived at the party. Roseanne's little wooden bungalow was already full of women. Someone thrust a glass of champagne at Amanda before she could remove her coat. Music thumped. The lights were covered in red cellophane. A spangled HAPPY BIRTHDAY banner fluttered against the sitting room wall. Apart from the stereo and a table weighed down with nibbles, Roseanne's furniture had vanished to make room for dancing.

Amanda glanced around. Everyone seemed to be in a couple. A hand touched her shoulder.

"Darling!" Roseanne kissed her on both cheeks and took the gift and the wine from her. Bright-eyed, she looked cute in a striped vest and green velvet pants Amanda hadn't seen before. "Come on down to the kitchen. Some of us are trying to have a conversation."

"Happy birthday," Amanda said, catching a speculative gleam from a dark-haired woman lighting a cigarette in the hallway.

In the kitchen Roseanne took her coat and jacket, "Sit down," she said. "Have some wine. I'll put these in my room."

A blond women with a ring through her top lip introduced herself as Imogen and said she was an industrial relations conciliator but she wanted to be a poet.

Amanda asked her how she knew Roseanne. Imogen said they'd only just met. She'd come to the party with a flatmate who was a friend of Roseanne's. She waved at a thin woman wearing a silver cocktail dress, fishnet stockings and Doc Marten ankle boots. "That's Lizzy, my muse," she said wistfully.

Several other women introduced themselves. Amanda gave her name and said nothing about her job. The conversation underway was on the ethics of euthanasia. A woman who was a nurse said she'd just reported herself to the police for administering a fatal dose of morphine at the request of a patient dying of AIDS. Now she was waiting to see if they would press charges.

Roseanne came back and said, "Look what I got!" She tilted her head from side to side displaying the amethyst and pearl drop earrings Amanda had agonized over. "Thank you." She dropped a kiss on Amanda's head.

"They're gorgeous," said Imogen, the would-be poet.

Past her shoulder Amanda caught the eye of the dark-haired woman smoking in the hallway.

Following her stare, Roseanne murmured, "That's Henry . . . Henrietta Dove, the novelist. Want to meet her?"

"I've never read anything she's written," Amanda said.

"Then you'll have to talk about the weather," Roseanne teased. Taking Amanda's hand she led her out of the kitchen, kissing various well-wishers and introducing Amanda in cringe-making terms as "the supercop you've all been busting to meet."

Mercifully she was more discreet with the delicious Henry Dove, merely suggesting the two had a great deal in common.

The writer murmured something in her ear and, laughing, Roseanne said, "I guessed as much. Have fun you two."

"I told her she must have read my mind," Henry informed Amanda in a low melodic voice. "I was hoping she'd bring you over."

"Really?" Amanda felt her pulse jump slightly.

Henry Dove was a few inches shorter than Amanda. Her skin was very pale against her dark hair and eyes, a striking look accentuated by her light foundation and scarlet lipstick. She might have been twenty-five. Or forty. "You're a detective, aren't you?" she said. "You shine a light into secret places and uncover hidden truths."

"That's one way to describe poking around in people's dirty linen," Amanda said.

"You know, writing novels isn't too glamorous

103

either." Henry took her arm and started walking toward the sitting room. She smelled of cinnamon. "There's nothing exciting about spending twelve hours a day crossing out every word that seemed ideal when you first thought of it."

"What kind of novels do you write?" Amanda raised her voice to be heard above the pounding music.

Henry's eyes crinkled. "You haven't read me? How refreshing." She leaned slightly into Amanda. "Why don't we talk about work later. Want to dance?"

Her accent was delicious, Amanda thought, recognizing a Scottish lilt. Smiling, she relaxed into the music. Roseanne was right. She needed to get out more.

They danced for nearly half an hour, until flushed and laughing they made their way to the makeshift bar in Roseanne's kitchen. Filling their glasses with ice and Coke, Amanda said, "Let's get some fresh air."

Roseanne had decorated her courtyard garden with tall yellow lanterns. In summer, fragrant jasmine trailed across trellis frames, competing with the splendid magnolias that screened the little house from its neighbors. Winter had laid everything bare. Skeletal branches shrouded the love seat in the far corner and the flower borders were piled high with fertilizer. Condensation dripped from every surface.

Henry lit a cigarette. "Fantastically cold, isn't it?"

Amanda looked up. For the first time in weeks

the sky was clear, the new moon buoyed on a sea of stars. "It's beautiful."

"I love Wellington," Henry said. "It's such an elemental place. Where I live you can watch the storms rolling in from the sea."

"Me too," Amanda said. "It's amazing how the wind comes up so suddenly and the sea gets choppy and changes color."

"You're in Evans Bay, aren't you?"

Surprised, Amanda said, "How did you know?"

"Roseanne told me. I think she's trying to set us up together."

This was the time to declare that she was someone else's girlfriend, Amanda thought. Except that she and Debby were nonmonogamous. In theory, anyway. "You're single?" she asked her companion.

"Celibate, actually. Of course Roseanne thinks there's no such thing and I must be pining."

Watching twists of smoke rise from Henry's cigarette, Amanda wondered what a one night stand would be like. Probably a fumbling disaster — two people under pressure to perform, neither knowing the other's body. Perhaps Henry didn't like sex, Amanda deliberated, or was "celibate" a euphemism for desperate?

Henry flicked ash into the garden. "Roseanne said you're in a long-distance relationship."

"We see each other when we can." Amanda felt awkward. "It's one of those no strings arrangements."

"You're not committed?"

Amanda wanted to answer no firmly and

positively. Instead she found herself chewing over the concept of commitment. You make a promise and you keep it. She had made no promises to Debby. She allowed herself to study Henry Dove's mouth. Definitely a kissable woman.

Henry caught her looking. "You haven't asked me why I'm celibate."

"You prefer flirting?" Amanda ventured.

Henry conceded this possibility with a small provocative smile. "You could find out." She turned her head sharply, staring toward the house. "Did you hear that?"

Prompted by the sound of something smashing, Amanda was already moving toward the back door. Above the music, women's voices sounded shrill and panicky. Pushing her way through the women in the kitchen, Amanda squeezed down the crowded hallway into Roseanne's sitting room. There, surrounded by horrorstruck faces, a woman wielding a broken bottle was circling the thin woman in the silver cocktail dress and Doc Martens.

Reaching for the power point, Amanda killed the music. "Get back," she yelled to the women around her.

The woman with the bottle registered surprise, but remained where she was.

"Put it down," Amanda ordered sternly. "Or someone's going to get hurt."

"Amanda . . ." Roseanne appeared beside her. "Be careful."

"Shift these women out of here," Amanda hissed. Advancing toward the woman with the bottle, she said, "You've made your point. Now back off."

She laughed. "You gonna make me?"

Stepping in front of the woman who was being menaced, Amanda pushed her back into the crowd. "I'm giving you one more chance," she said. "Drop it now."

The woman with the bottle responded with a mock feint.

"Amanda . . . please," Roseanne begged. "I don't want a scene. Just take it off her and throw her out."

She was short, slightly unsteady on her feet. Amanda kept her eyes on the bottle. "Don't be stupid," she warned. "I'm a police officer."

"Yeah, right."

It was so simple, Amanda thought. A sudden forward movement, a step sideways. The woman tried to swing the bottle back around, but Amanda caught her arm and lowered it with a crack against her knee. The bottle flew from her fingers. Kicking the broken glass aside, Amanda jerked the woman's arm sharply behind her back and kicked her legs out, pushing her face down on the floor. Pinning her there, she ordered Roseanne, "Go get my coat. There's some handcuffs in the pocket."

Roseanne looked stupefied.

"Do it," Amanda yelled. Shoving her ID under the prone woman's face, she said, "You are under arrest." As she read her rights and informed her she was charged with assault and disorderly conduct, she was conscious of a sea of shocked faces.

Roseanne, pale and shaking, returned with the cuffs. "Please," she murmured, as Amanda secured the woman's wrists. "Is this really necessary. She is just a drunk idiot making a scene."

"Are you telling me to let her go?"

Roseanne looked miserable. "It's my birthday party."

"She was assaulting one of your guests."

The woman in the silver dress said, "Look, I don't want to press charges. She just got upset over something I said."

Frustrated, Amanda lifted the woman to her feet.

"I was just having you on." The woman in the silver dress was acting like she was the one who needed to apologize. "C'mon, Mel."

Amanda stared at the woman she'd cuffed. "What's your name?"

The woman said nothing.

"Mel Carter," Roseanne answered for her.

Amanda smiled. "I was hoping you'd say that."

CHAPTER TEN

Mel Carter was sitting in the interview room with her feet on the table. At first she ignored Amanda and Gibbs, then she lowered her feet to the floor. "Your coffee's fucking awful," she commented, rolling her sleeves up to display elaborate tattoos on her forearms. Catching Amanda's passing glance, she jibed, "What's wrong, Inspector? Scared of the big bad dyke?"

Amanda held back a laugh. Mel was not much over five-foot-three, her build compact and solid, molded by leather pants and vest. Her hair was short, flat across the top and gelled into bristles, a style which accentuated her squarish face. Its natural color was probably light brown, but right now it was black, a choice that made her skin seem sallow but heightened the impact of her pale blue eyes.

The doctor had found her to be sober, and according to the register, the police had removed from her person one set of handcuffs, a studded wristband, a whistle, a short-handled leather whip, a set of studded leather knuckle dusters and two objects the bewildered sergeant had termed "rubber device" and "leather device."

"Like what you see?" Mel taunted quietly.

What Amanda saw was an insecure woman with a carefully cultivated image. "Melanie Carter . . ." she mused aloud. "Catholic girl?"

Mel's eyes flickered. "What's it to you?"

Amanda yawned. "Got that witness statement typed up yet, Sergeant?"

Gibbs vanished for a moment then returned, perspiring, a thick file clutched in one of his fleshy hands. Scowling and slouching, he could have passed for nightclub bouncer — bulldog neck, square jaw, scarred face. Perfect, she thought. Exactly the impression she'd asked him for.

Browsing the papers in leisurely silence, she was conscious of Mel's feet shuffling beneath the table. There was nothing worse than being the center of attention, only to find yourself ignored.

"Quite a pedigree," Amanda directed her comment at Gibbs. "Assault, reckless driving causing injury, willful damage . . ."

Gibbs' gaze traveled edgily around the small room. "Those are just the convictions."

"Feeling okay, Sergeant?" Amanda asked him in a sympathetic tone. "Still having problems with that claustrophobia?"

Gibbs said he was fine. He managed to look completely unhinged.

"Excellent," Amanda made like she didn't notice a thing. "Please continue."

Obligingly Gibbs reeled off Mel's rights, verified her name and personal details, and told her she was entitled to request a legal representative.

Mel shot an uneasy look at Amanda. "What the hell is he talking about? I don't need a lawyer. I haven't done anything."

"Just answer the questions," Amanda said.

Gibbs recorded the subject as using foul language, then began to pace. "Sexual violation. That's a serious charge. With a previous like yours, you'll do a stretch. Ten years maybe." He allowed that to sink in.

"I don't believe this!" Mel threw Amanda a belligerent look.

Amanda appeared engrossed in the file she was holding. "Carry on, Sergeant," she said in a disinterested tone.

"We have an eye witness statement from a friend of yours, Jolene Ruth, linking you to the sexual assault of a Ms. Sara Hart between the hours of five and seven on Wednesday night." Gibbs stared her down. "So don't waste my time or the Inspector's telling lies as to your whereabouts."

Mel seemed riveted by the grim working of his scar.

He plunged on. "We know you carried out a cowardly attack on a defenseless young female. What have you got to say for yourself?"

"Oh I get it." Mel swung a sharp glance to Amanda. "The old good-cop bad-cop routine. You pigs are so original."

She had barely finished her sentence when Gibbs seized the back of her chair, jerking it round to face him. "Apologize to the Inspector, you scumbag," he shouted, inches from her face.

Mel seemed frozen, the bravado seeping from her face. Craning to see Amanda, she complained, "This guy's crazy . . ."

Amanda shrugged. "Comes with the job."

"Yeah, I spend too much time cleaning up after trash like you." Gibbs kicked Mel's chair back into position and resumed his nervous pacing.

"There are laws against police harassment," Mel declared. "I don't have to take this homophobic crap — I'm going to report you to the Human Rights Commission."

"I'm sure the Commissioner will be thrilled," Amanda said. "You'll be their first equal opportunity rapist."

Mel groaned. "I told you. This is all bullshit. Jolene's my ex. She's pissed at me for fucking another woman —"

"You admit you had sex with Ms. Hart?"

"Yes, we had sex."

"Did Ms. Hart consent?"

"Of course she did. It was all set up ahead of time."

112

"Really?" According to Sara, she hadn't seen Mel since their brief encounter in Caspers bar two weeks ago. "When did you make these arrangements?"

Mel scratched her head. "Couple of weeks ago. At Caspers."

"When did you invite Jolene along?"

"We got talking last week. I told her Sara was hot for a scene and she said she'd be a starter." Mel had the grace to look uncomfortable. "Maybe it was a dumb idea. I mean, Jolene had it in for Sara. She's the jealous type. Know what I mean?"

"No, I don't." Amanda could guess, but she wanted Mel to say it on tape. "What was Jolene's role exactly?"

"She said she just wanted to watch, but she got right into it. Shit ..." Mel examined her tattoo, her body language defensive. "I probably should have stopped her, right. I mean, the stuff with the cigarettes was pretty sick. I told her to knock that off ..."

Amanda exchanged a look with Gibbs. "Sara said she tried to stop what was happening, but you wouldn't listen. Didn't you arrange some kind of safe word with her?"

Mel looked completely blank.

Her history as a leather person was as old as her brand new gear, Amanda surmised. Recalling Jolene's comment about Mel's appearance being a "fashion thing," she asked, "Do you know anyone who practices sadomasochism, Mel?"

Mel gave a brassy shrug. "I've seen them around."

"And it's a look you like?"

"Yeah. Gets the girls interested."

"You think it got Sara interested?"

Mel grinned. "She could hardly keep her knees together. I don't know what bullshit she's told you, but this was all her idea. She was the one with the fantasy. She wanted it."

"Then why did she ask you to stop?"

"It was part of the game." Mel broke off. "You wouldn't understand."

"Try me."

Mel's eyes smoldered. "Is that an invitation?" Lowering her voice, she leaned forward so that only Amanda could hear her. "I think the newspapers might want to know what you were doing at a lesbian party tonight, Inspector."

"Then I'd better release a press statement," Amanda replied.

Mel shifted in her chair. "Look," she whined. "What's it to you what I do in the bedroom? Dear little Sara wanted to be tied up. Is that a fucking crime? I slapped her around some, and she begged for more. Satisfied?"

The doctor's report listed bruising and lacerations consistent with an extended beating. Sara Hart had been punched, kicked, whipped, slapped and burnt with cigarette butts. One of her nipples was torn, her vagina was lacerated, two of her ribs were broken.

"She begged for more," Amanda slowly repeated. "Was that before or after you gagged her?"

Mel was silent, her jaw set.

"How much alcohol did you drink that night?" Amanda asked.

Mel looked uncertain, perhaps trying to figure out whether the male excuse of drunken irresponsibility, accompanied by convincing remorse, would work for her.

Don't waste your time, Amanda felt like saying. Drunken rape and pillage were still tacitly legitimized by the courts and an indulgent media as men "letting off steam." But women were unlikely to receive similar carte blanche. Amanda pictured a brawling all-female gang smashing up cars and vandalizing houses on their way home from a netball match. They'd bring in the army.

"I had a few beers," Mel admitted.

"What time did you leave Ms. Hart's flat?" Gibbs asked.

"Christ, how would I know? It was dark."

"You left alone?"

"No." Mel didn't hesitate. "With Jolene."

"Where did you go then?" Gibbs asked briskly.

"To Jolene's."

"Who else was there?"

"One of her flatmates . . . can't remember her name. Flaky type with a scarf wrapped round her head. She made us a cup of tea."

"You left Sara tied up naked on the floor of her kitchen," Amanda said. "Weren't you worried something might go wrong. She could have frozen . . . got into breathing difficulties . . ."

Mel scratched her head. For the first time in the interview she looked abashed. "Yeah. I told Jolene we shouldn't leave the gag on. But she said the flatmate would get home soon and find her. I rang the number later on to make sure. I hung up as soon as the flatmate answered."

"Where were you when you made that call?"

"Jolene's. I spent the night there."

"Whose idea was that?"

Mel seemed smug. "Let's just say Jolene was kind of worked up after everything."

Amanda was conscious of the faint hiss of the tape, the heat from the light overhead. Mel seemed to have no idea how serious her situation was. Corroboration would sort out the glaring discrepancies between her account of events and Jolene's, but Amanda was in no doubt which woman a jury would believe.

"Mel," she said, earning a look of faint surprise from Gibbs. "You're being questioned on a very serious charge. I advise you to think again about talking to a lawyer."

"Look, there's no law against sex in this country," Mel insisted. "Why should I have to pay some lawyer to say that?"

"Sex isn't the issue," Amanda said. "The issue is consent."

"Fucking Jolene. That stupid little bitch." Mel absently popped her knuckles. "I didn't do anything wrong. Ask Sara."

Amanda watched her face closely. "We have."

Mel's expression did not alter. "What did she say?"

"That you raped her."

"Shit." Mel folded her arms across her body. "I don't get it."

"What do you think?" Amanda poured coffee into two cups and handed one to Gibbs.

"Cunning as a bag of rats or plain stupid. Either way, she'll go down." Gibbs stirred sugar into his coffee. "What do you want to do about Jolene Ruth? Obviously her lawyer is looking to deal."

Amanda brushed spilled sugar off her desk and wished she'd never got herself involved. This was shaping to be one of those quicksand cases that sucked everyone down with it. "I'll interview Sara again," she said. "You take two detectives — Brody and Bergman, and see what you can corroborate. If we can find someone who saw the two women leaving together, we'll charge Jolene on all counts."

Gibbs looked dubious. "That could be a mistake. That lawyer of hers will make Hart look like some kind of nymphomaniac psych case. But if we run with Ruth as a prosecution witness, Carter will do time. One out of two . . . it's not bad." He tortured the edges of his Styrofoam cup. "Incredible. You half expect it from a bloke . . . she wanted it . . . all the usual crap. Works like self-hypnosis. In the end, they'll pass a lie detector test because they've persuaded themselves it wasn't rape. Some of them really believe it."

"They want to believe it," Amanda said.

Gibbs closed Mel's file and placed it on Amanda's desk. "So does she. That's what I'm saying . . . you don't expect a woman to kid herself like that, about another woman."

Amanda's throat felt harsh. We do it all the time, she thought. "People believe what they want to believe," she mouthed the cliché automatically.

"No jury will believe Carter," Gibbs said.

* * * * *

117

Lucky? Tiddles? Onyx?

"Kitty, kitty . . ." Amanda stretched her hand out to the black cat stalking around the kitchen.

From the living room, Madam made a throaty objection, tail switching.

"Show some compassion," Amanda said. "This house is big enough for the three of us."

Madam pointedly lost interest and clawed the sofa. Amanda threw a terry towel at her. The new cat stared at the refrigerator and purred. Succumbing, Amanda fed her a second helping of steak and kidney. The phone rang and she grabbed it, heart thudding. Two in the morning. What was the time in Rwanda?

"Amanda?" Roseanne sounded tearful.

Swallowing disappointment, Amanda said stiffly, "What's up?"

A pause. "Can I come 'round?"

"I'm tired."

"Me too. But I can't sleep." Her voice sounded thick with alcohol. "What are you doing?"

"I just got home."

"You don't want to see me?"

"Yes," Amanda tried to soften her tone. "But not now, Rosy. Okay?"

Roseanne sniffed. "I'm sorry I got mad at you. I know you have to do your job."

"I had to take her in," Amanda said. "We had a warrant out for her. She's facing other charges."

Roseanne blew her nose. "It was my birthday. I just wanted everything to be perfect."

"Get some sleep," Amanda said. "You'll feel better in the morning." She could hear Roseanne breathing at the other end of the phone. "I still love you."

Roseanne made a small choking noise. "Me too. 'Bye."

Amanda listened to the dial tone for a moment. Roseanne was not in the habit of making phone calls at two in the morning. Or quitting her job. Or getting drunk.

Amanda phoned her back. She got the answer machine. "Are you there, Rosy?" she asked as the message tape ran. "Come on over if you want. You know where the key is."

She rang off and went upstairs. In the shower, lightheaded all of a sudden, she realized she hadn't eaten all day.

CHAPTER ELEVEN

From the air, Australia looked like a huge red picnic cloth floating on a hazy ocean. The first time Amanda visited the place, several years ago, she had expected strange pouched animals, gumtrees, billabongs and people who wore leather hats and spoke a vernacular that may as well have been another language. Instead she had found herself in Melbourne, a cosmopolitan city with three million people of 140 nationalities, and more restaurants, espresso bars and trees per square mile than virtually any city in the world.

The outback existed. Carolyn Stuart, a friend she'd made at a forensic science convention five years ago, had obligingly driven her there. It was dry, red and smelled of eucalyptus. The heat was unbearable. The only people who could survive the unique terrain were the Aboriginal tribes, or what was left of them after two hundred years of discreet genocide. Occasionally they rescued lost tourists who, with the gung-ho of those who knew absolutely nothing but had a wallet full of credit cards, fancied they could hire a jeep and take a short cut to Ayres Rock.

Since the convention, Amanda and Carolyn had kept in touch, writing and visiting each other occasionally.

"You couldn't have picked a worse time to come over," Carolyn said, as they crossed the airport parking lot sharing an umbrella. "It hasn't stopped raining in days, it's the football season, and I'm involved in the divorce case from hell." She halted at a shiny blue-black Saab and unlocked the trunk. " I know you're not here voluntarily, so what's the story?"

"It's a homicide," Amanda said. "The victim was Bryce Petty. He was president of some gay and lesbian TV station —"

"Spectrum," Carolyn interjected. "How amazing. I know all about it. That divorce case I'm working on . . . it's the wife."

Amanda frowned. "You've lost me."

"The politician who sued them. His wife's divorcing him. She's my client."

"I see." Amanda saw absolutely nothing.

"He was awarded half a million in damages and his people are refusing to include it in his assets for the settlement," Carolyn explained. "Naturally, I'm going to fry their asses. Her reputation suffered just as much damage as his, although that's not the point, of course." She kept up a steady monologue as they passed acres of suburban real estate development, telling Amanda that Spectrum was the biggest scandal to hit gay and lesbian Melbourne since the police raid on the Tasty nightclub. "You ought to talk to a mate of mine — Chloe Furness," Carolyn said. "She was directing the current affairs show that caused all the trouble. I wonder if she knows he's dead." Stretching an arm down beside her seat, she wrestled her handbag onto her knee, extracted a cellular phone and punched in some numbers.

As Amanda contemplated taking over the wheel, Carolyn held the phone to her ear with one hand and steered with the other, talking at a frantic pace to a person Amanda assumed to be Chloe, the director.

"That's illegal," Amanda said when Carolyn dropped the mobile back into her handbag. "Besides which, you could kill yourself."

"Live fast. Die young. What can I say?"

She looked tired, Amanda thought, noting the strained set of her mouth, her shadowed gray eyes. Always slender, she seemed brittle, her movements lacking the fluid grace Amanda had found so appealing the first time they met. Like Amanda, Carolyn was a single-minded achiever, an attorney who had made plain her ambition to become a judge eventually. She would turn forty very soon, this maturity enhancing her prospects of reaching the bench. The most recent sacrifice she had made to her career was her relationship of nine years.

Sally had been restless for a while, Amanda recalled. She and Carolyn had talked of couples counseling and space apart. "How are you?" She tried for a light tone, attempting to disguise the subtext — *are you coping? Is there any chance of a reconciliation?*

Carolyn shrugged, jaw tensing, gaze fixed on the road. "I'll survive."

Therapy had never been Amanda's forte. "I like your car," she said, escaping into neutral territory. "How long have you had it?"

"Three weeks." Carolyn gave a small mechanical laugh. "I bought it the day I saw them together. It was ridiculous really . . ." She trailed off, negotiating her way from the Tullamarine Freeway into the slow-moving city traffic. "They were just sitting there in the Angel Café, gazing at each other. I didn't even notice them at first. I was eating by myself. Then I heard Sally laugh. I felt like blowing their heads off."

"Some people settle for a tattoo when they break up," Amanda murmured.

"Not me. I'm into serious pain, in the wallet department. Besides, I needed a new car. She took ours."

Carolyn lived in a leafy cul-de-sac in East St. Kilda. Her ground-floor apartment bordered on luxury, its plain walls and carpeting set off by rich soft furnishings and equally bright modern paintings. She had bought Sally out, Amanda assumed, noting the absence of an antique chiffonnier she had always liked. Sally had taken it when they split the furniture, she supposed.

Dropping her coat and satchel on an armchair, Carolyn said. "I've swapped things around a bit so we have a proper guest room." She led Amanda down a hallway to the room that had been Sally's study. Amanda had vague memories of dark bookshelves, brocade curtains and washable wallpaper. The room was now a pastel masterpiece in shades of dove gray and apricot, with Laura Ashley overtones.

"It's charming," Amanda managed, scanning the elaborate bedding, lace window dressing and reproduction Queen Anne dressing table. Carolyn had really cut loose. After nine years with a woman who insisted on ergonomics and durable colors, the femme within had busted out.

"As you can see my mother has left her usual indelible mark on the decor," Carolyn said dryly. "She wanted to help."

That was nice, Amanda thought. Carolyn and her mother seemed to have a comfortable relationship. Mrs. Stuart had always been accepting of her daughter's lesbianism, in fact seemed to applaud it. Carolyn was apparently her favorite, the only girl in a family of four boys.

She had always been encouraged by her parents, she'd told Amanda. This was so unusual in the ultra-sexist Australia of her childhood that friends of the family had been appalled, imagining her parents would create a monster.

"I'll put the kettle on while you unpack," Carolyn said. Hovering in the doorway, she added. "I'm sorry I'm like this. It's really good to see you."

She was devastated, she told Amanda an hour

later. They were on their third Scotch. Wrestling with inhibitions about sloshing down alcohol like it was Snapple, Amanda put her glass firmly on the coffee table beside her and told herself to make it last.

Carolyn gazed worriedly at the depleted bottle. "Tell me if I'm getting loud, won't you?"

The story was sordid. Weren't they all? Amanda thought. At least when another woman was involved. Sally, who had returned to school to complete her master's, had fallen for a lecturer, Lana Godfrey. The woman was some kind of feminist icon, the writer of a controversial book called *Transgressive Deconstruction: A Lesbian Cultural Discourse*. Amanda had never heard of it, or the author. "I don't get the time to read that political stuff," she commented. "Criminology's my area."

"You'd know the jacket," Carolyn assured her. "Most people buy it for that. Actually, I've read some of her work. She raises a few interesting issues. I guess we need to bring this stuff out in the open . . . get debate going."

"Sure." Amanda wondered who "we" represented. Academics, she supposed. Who else had the time, unless they were unemployed?

"But I can't agree with some of the strategies she recommends." Carolyn poured herself another drink. "And I don't think she's really interested in genuine debate. Lana Godfrey's opinions are facts. That's how she frames everything. There's no room for interpretation. She's right. Full stop." She stared into her glass. "I can't believe Sally fell for her. Lana's not her type at all."

"Is she, er . . ." Amanda tried to fathom some way

of saying *great looking* or *accomplished in the sack* without sounding as if she thought Carolyn were lacking in either department.

"Gorgeous?" Carolyn was a jump ahead, always the lawyer. "In a word, no. She's forty-three, scrawny, makes a virtue out of bad hairdos and sweaty armpits. I don't know what she spends her salary on, but it's not her wardrobe."

Amanda had never heard Carolyn make such harsh personal remarks about another woman. Clearly the gloves were off. "When did it start?" she asked.

"I don't know for sure. They pretended nothing was happening, but I caught them here one day. In our bed." Grimly cynical. "Having, er . . . cultural discourse."

"I'm sorry," Amanda said.

Carolyn gave a weary sigh. "Me too. Well, that was bad enough but there's more."

What else could they do? Public humiliation — a wedding at the Metropolitan Church perhaps?

"Sally begged me to keep quiet about the affair," Carolyn went on. "Lana was with someone else at the time and her partner had just inherited quite a lot of money. She needed to pay off some debts and she wanted them to buy a joint property together, so she could claim it after the break-up."

Responding to Amanda's gasp, she said, "I know. It's disgusting, isn't it? So basically they blackmailed me. I had to keep quiet or Sally would go to some women's magazine and spill her guts about our relationship. Can you imagine it?"

Amanda nodded slowly. Carolyn was deeply closeted and intended to remain so until she achieved her ambition to be appointed as a judge.

"I buckled," she said bitterly. "I did exactly what they wanted. I pretended everything was just fine while they were carrying on all the time. I know I was a fool but I kept hoping it was some kind of crazy phase and Sally would work her way through it."

"When did she leave?"

"Six weeks ago. Remember this?" She went to her desk and returned with a familiar sheet of lavender paper.

Amanda scanned the contents. Headed up *Dear Friends and Family*, the note said, *Carolyn and Sally have decided to live apart. We're sad about this, but it was a mutual decision. Recently, we've found we have less and less in common and our goals are taking us in different directions. We've therefore decided to go our separate ways.*

"I thought your job was to blame," Amanda said. She could relate to that.

"It was my idea to write the letter," Carolyn said. "Our anniversary came along and I just couldn't go on living that farce. I even started to think about killing myself. Then I thought why the hell should I? So I sent one of these to everyone, including Sally." She laughed, then started to cry. "I don't understand how she could hurt me like that. That's what I can't accept. It was so cruel. I feel so betrayed."

Amanda held her. She and Debby had done the right thing, she decided. This was exactly the kind of mess they were avoiding.

CHAPTER TWELVE

Outside Amanda's window, a raucous parrot barked its distinctive cry at the indecisive morning sun. Rubbing her dehydrated eyes, Amanda dragged herself out of bed. She had an hour to collect her thoughts, then she was meeting Detective Sergeant Mary Devine to discuss the Petty case. Selecting black gabardine pants and a plaid jacket from her suit carrier, she turned on the shower.

Twenty minutes later she was drinking coffee with Carolyn who had just returned from an hour of power walking. "Look at this." She slid a gay newspaper across the table to Amanda.

A banner headline on the front page blared MISSING SPECTRUM PRESIDENT DEAD. There followed a potted history of the case and speculative comment on Petty's disappearance and subsequent murder. Spectrum Vice-President India Niall was "unavailable for comment," but someone called Lou Riddell was quoted as saying the killing came as "no surprise to the people Mr. Petty had ripped off" and that "insiders have their own theories about who did it."

"Sounds like this Riddell guy is angling for an interview." Amanda folded the paper and shoved it into her satchel.

"How long do you think you'll be here?" Carolyn asked.

"Just a few days, I hope. I'm meeting with a couple of Melbourne detectives this morning to plan the investigation at this end. As far as I'm concerned they can take over."

Carolyn toyed with her cup. "You're welcome to stay on a bit, if you want."

"I need to get back," Amanda said. "I'm on another case."

"I'm sorry about last night. I didn't plan to dump on you the minute you walked off the plane." Carolyn cleared away the breakfast dishes and set her answer machine. Folding her coat over her arm, she flicked a darting glance at Amanda. "I . . . I was wondering if you'd like to eat out tonight. Leo's Spaghetti Bar is just down the road . . ."

She seemed oddly tentative. Hoping she didn't feel

obliged to entertain her, Amanda said, "Sure. But if you have other plans, I can look after myself."

"No. I'd only be eating junk food and watching the tube." Carolyn took her car keys from a hook beside the telephone. "Want a lift down to the station?"

Amanda shook her head. "Thanks, but I'll take a taxi later on. I have some things to do here."

"I'll see you then." Carolyn waved from the doorway.

There was an odd tension about her smile that unsettled Amanda. It was nothing, she thought, pouring herself another coffee. There had never been the slightest attraction between her and Carolyn, and for her part that hadn't changed. She hoped it was the same for Carolyn.

Detective Sergeant Mary Devine was not exactly thrilled to see Amanda. Shifting a mountain of papers from the chair beside her desk, she said, "I imagine you're aware that this case is not a high priority for us."

"Because Petty was gay?" Amanda asked up front.

Mary Devine offered her a cigarette and when she declined, dropped the packet on her desk without taking one. "We couldn't give a damn who Petty bonked," she said, flicking through a dog-eared notebook. "He was killed in your sandpit, not ours."

Statistics, Amanda thought. The credit for solving the case would belong to Wellington CIB regardless of Melbourne's input. And there would be no joyrides across the Tasman for the Australian detectives.

"The father's your prime suspect, right?" Mary said.

"So far we can't link him to the scene —"

"But he wanted his money back?"

"The son also had a big insurance policy," Amanda said.

"So Dad whacks him, gets back what he lent plus a dividend?" Mary chewed on her pencil. "He can't be the only person looking to dance on Petty's grave."

"There's India Niall, the woman jointly responsible for paying the damages in the Spectrum lawsuit."

"Must have made her day when Petty pissed off with the money," Mary said. "She'd be up for the full five hundred, wouldn't she?"

Amanda handed over the clipping she'd taken from Carolyn's paper. "Seen this?"

Mary nodded. "Yeah. Got Lou Riddell stamped all over it. Your classic time waster. Self-appointed spokesperson for every queer committee this side of the black stump."

"I'd like to interview him."

"Her," Mary corrected. "She's post-op. I'm sure she'll be thrilled to see *you*." Without explaining herself, she dropped the pencil and reached for her cigarettes, impatiently lighting up. "I've gone through the data you faxed over. Any progress on the murder weapon?"

"I wish," Amanda said.

"Shame you couldn't execute a search warrant on the father. What's he like?"

"Self-righteous type. Treats his wife like shit."

"Fine Australian tradition," Mary remarked. Her

131

eyes were beautiful, Amanda noted. Dark hazel, hard to say whether they were green or brown. Her mouth bore traces of wine-colored lipstick. Amanda guessed she applied it once in the morning and after lunch. She didn't seem the type to check herself constantly in a mirror.

"I'd like to wrap this one up as soon as I can," Amanda said, sensitive to her Australian counterpart's workload.

"Join the club." Mary drew on her cigarette and exhaled very slowly. "Let's see what that old windbag Riddell's got for us, shall we?"

Mary was right. Lou Riddell was thrilled to see them. Examining their identification with an air of breathless self-importance, she ushered them into her office at the Melbourne Gay and Lesbian Charities Trust and posted a *Do Not Disturb* sign on the door.

Amanda tried to remember the last time she had seen a beehive hairdo as impressive as the one before her now. Miami, Florida. The family vacation in 1969, a couple of years before her mother left them.

"Tea, anybody?" Lou Riddell huskily invited. "It's Earl Grey."

"White. No sugar," Mary said.

Amanda declined.

"One of the girls can fetch you a take-out espresso, if you'd rather," Lou hovered at the door, her tone coquettish. "I know what you coffee drinkers are like."

Amanda caught an I-told-you-so glance from Mary,

who said, when Lou returned with the teapot, "I guess you know what we're here for, Lou."

Smoothing her beige twinset over her hips, their subject took a sip of her tea, little finger daintily crooked. Her expression was smug. "Bryce Petty," she said.

"You knew him well?" Amanda asked.

"Oh, yes. All the Spectrum people, actually. Their offices were on the floor downstairs."

"According to the newspapers you can virtually name the killer," Mary said dryly. "Is that bullshit, or is there something you should be telling us?"

Lou tossed her head like a pinup girl. Her double chin wobbled. "That silly little reporter *had* to exaggerate, of course. But I can tell you plenty. Guess who was in New Zealand when it happened . . . Pat Degrassi." She spat the name as if it tasted foul, then perceiving no reaction, explained, "That's India Niall's big butch girlfriend."

"Why would she have killed Bryce Petty?" Mary asked bluntly.

"Because she said she would. Because of the money."

"You personally heard her threaten Mr. Petty?" Amanda asked.

"Not in so many words." Lou patted her candyfloss hair. "But everyone knows how she felt about him."

"I gather she wasn't alone." Looking distinctly unimpressed, Mary said, "You're wasting our time, Lou."

"No. Wait. There's more." In her anxiety to detain them, Lou slopped tea into her saucer. "It's India . . . she's taken her house off the market."

133

"Really?" Expressionless, Mary opened the door.

"She doesn't need to sell it now. They say she's paid her share of the damages. Who knows where she got the money from."

"Where do you think?" Amanda asked.

"Her girlfriend got it off Bryce before she killed him," Lou declared, clutching at her wattled throat. "You don't have to be Einstein to figure that out."

On the floor below, Spectrum's sign was still on the door of the office suite. A handwritten notice taped across it referred inquiries to the accountancy firm in charge of liquidation.

"They've had the place sealed off since the court case," Mary said, wielding a set of keys. "But the accountant was very helpful when I called. We can photocopy anything we need."

Amanda entered the deserted reception area. Notices on a board listed production courses for volunteers, and a collection of newspaper clippings marked various highlights in Spectrum's short history. One of them featured a cherubic Bryce Petty accepting a community service award.

"We could start with the management committee minutes," Mary said. "See who came to meetings . . ." She handed Amanda a bound volume. "Correspondence is probably worth a look, too."

Amanda scanned a few pages of minutes. Predictably dull. Going back six months, a name jumped out at her. Pat Degrassi had been on the management committee. But not for long. After a few pages, there was a curt record of her resignation and that of the committee secretary. The reason cited for both was "other commitments."

Over successive pages, the minutes became little more than an attendance record. Apparently no one had been voted in to replace the secretary or Degrassi. Amanda jotted down the names of everyone who had attended meetings. To her surprise, a register naively listed the addresses and phone numbers of all Spectrum members. Even in this liberal part of the world she would have expected such information to be confidential.

"Apparently Spectrum's finances were in a total shambles," Mary said. "The accountant told me they would have gone under, whether or not they were sued . . . inept management."

Amanda returned the register to its shelf. A lot of people had obviously put energy into Spectrum, she thought. It was a shame it had all been for nothing.

Their discussion with private investigator Patrick Ryan, half an hour later, was equally discouraging. The guy ran an agency in Richmond, his offices a musty set of rooms sandwiched between two restaurants in the area known as Little Vietnam.

Warning them that time was money and since the police weren't paying he wouldn't be doing their job for them, Ryan reluctantly showed Mary and Amanda into his airless office. His chair dominated the room, a towering black leather swivel job with adjustable arms and headrest, and a cantilever attachment for holding the phone to his ear. He plopped into this, his stomach overflowing into his lap. Sweat rings glued his shirt to his armpits.

"Petty . . . yeah, I got it here." Resting his cigarette on an ashtray, he tinkered on his computer for a moment. "The mother hired me. Not a Catholic, but a nice lady all the same. Wanted me to trace the son. Money for old rope."

"Did she say why she was looking for him?" Mary asked.

"None of my business, sweetheart." He jabbed the screen. "It says here family matter. That can mean any fucking thing in this line of work, pardon my language. You oughta know that."

"Are you aware that Mr. Petty was murdered last week?" Amanda said.

"That a fact?" He acted surprised. "She wasted her dough then. Shame about that."

A buzzer sounded and Ryan's famished looking receptionist opened the door, announcing that a Mrs. O'Grady had arrived.

"Adultery," Ryan informed them, retrieving his cigarette and getting to his feet. "You don't turn it down."

Mary handed her card over. "If you think of anything . . ."

"The husband rang me. Tried to cancel the job." He flicked the card absently onto a pile of paperwork. "Bad-tempered bastard."

"How do you mean?" Mary asked.

"Had Kylie in tears." He jerked a thumb toward reception. "Came up here yelling and ranting. I was out at the time, more's the pity."

"But you spoke to him in the end?"

"Oh, yeah. Told him he was too late. She'd already got the address."

"When was that?" Amanda asked.

"Must be a month ago, at least." He held the door open for them. "If you're talking to Mrs. Petty, tell I'm sorry about her boy. She wanted to find him real bad. I remember that."

Mary seemed to be asking herself mental questions and answering them all the way back to the station. She had cleared a spare desk near hers for Amanda. Flimsy partitioning did nothing to reduce the noise level from the surrounding areas. On the phone to Austin Shaw, Amanda stuck a finger in her ear to block out the sound of an argument going on a few feet away. Someone had left his car in the wrong space and it had been towed.

"How's your mother?" she asked Shaw.

"Doing pretty well. Her doctor seems to think they got everything."

"Good." Her ear hurt.

"I think we've traced that Mitsubishi," he said. "Looks like a rental car." He would fax Amanda a list of all the white rentals that were out on the day of the killing.

"Anything on the weapon?"

"No. And we're nowhere with the trace. All the blood in the apartment is Petty's group. The prints belong to him and Awatere. There's a few unidentified latents ... probably belong to the tradesmen who decorated the place. But there are some wool fibers that don't match any clothing of his."

They'd also checked out Mrs. Petty's story, he said. She was verified as a passenger on a six thirty commuter flight from Rotorua to Tauranga. Apparently she'd been on a scenic day tour of Rotorua, leaving Taupo at nine that morning. They had her reservation records and the bus company had confirmed she was a passenger.

"If anyone has something to hide it's the father," he said.

"That list of rental cars . . ."

"His name's not on it. Going to the funeral tomorrow?"

"Looks that way," Amanda muttered. "Ruling out divine intervention."

"Take in the opera while you're in town," he recommended. "It's Joan Carden in *Tosca*."

"Fabulous." Amanda pictured Jim Petty washing his son's blood off his hands, pulling a coat over his splattered clothing. Where had he dumped everything? "Anything turn up in Petty's hotel room?" she asked.

"Moira's in there today."

"One speck of blood and we've got him," Amanda said.

"What chance of a search warrant at your end?"

The Australian police tended to be more generous in their interpretation of probable cause than their New Zealand counterparts, but with the homicide going down off-shore and nothing to connect Petty to the scene, Amanda was not optimistic. "I'll see what I can do."

Perhaps Petty would relax a little now he was back home and let something slip to his wife. Gripped by a sudden unease, Amanda thought about Mrs. Petty limping toward the elevator, her husband having declined the offer of a ride. Apparently he took her loyalty for granted. How far would he go to protect himself if he had cause to doubt her?

Farewelling Austin Shaw, Amanda put the phone down and checked the paper in the fax machine. She and Mary had arranged to see India Niall that afternoon. They could make a routine call on the Pettys on their way back, she decided. The gumshoe, Patrick Ryan, had got her thinking. If Mrs. Petty had known for weeks where her son was, why hadn't she told her husband?

Sipping her takeout espresso, she covertly studied Mary Devine. The detective looked a little older than her, thirty-six maybe. She was about the same height, but fuller in the breasts and hips. Her hair was dark brown, waves just brushing her shoulders. She had it bunched back behind her ears while she worked, revealing small lobes adorned with pearl studs. A shaft of sunlight leaked through the venetian blinds, casting shifting patterns on her face. Feeling a small, sharp jolt of attraction, Amanda wondered if she was married.

At that moment Mary looked up, commenting, "Interesting. According to the court, the full amount of damages was paid this morning."

"Really? By whom?"

"Pat Degrassi." Mary looked intrigued.

The fax machine beeped into life and started scrolling pages of computer printout. Amanda stapled them together, quickly scanning the transactions. Her pulse jumped a beat. Two days before Petty was murdered a white Mitsubishi had been hired to a Patricia Degrassi. It was returned to the airport hire center the evening of the killing.

"Got something?" Mary came over and read across Amanda's shoulder.

Amanda circled Degrassi's name in red. "I sure hope so."

CHAPTER THIRTEEN

"She's off her face," Mary Devine murmured in Amanda's ear. "Prozac for breakfast, lunch and dinner — that's my guess."

India Niall had left them sitting in a cluttered sunroom while she took a phone call from her girlfriend. She returned, distractedly smoking a cigarette. "Want one?" she waved the packet around.

Declining, Mary said, "You must be relieved about the house — not having to sell, after all."

India took a couple of sharp puffs, and waved the smoke away. She looked about sixteen years old, in tight faded jeans and a huge sweater, her honey blond hair falling out of a ponytail. "We only bought the place last year."

"Bad business, this Spectrum thing..."

"Do we have to talk about that?" India grimaced. "It's all in the past now. I'm putting it behind me. Things to do... places to go."

"You would have been up for the whole lot if Bryce had got away with his dad's money, I guess," Mary persisted. "Five hundred grand."

India cast an edgy look toward the door. "It would have wiped us out. The house. The business. Everything."

"Did you know the liability risks when you were elected?" Mary asked.

"I guess I did. In theory." India stared into the smoke rising from her cigarette. "There were four of us at first, so it didn't seem so bad..."

"Why didn't you elect new office bearers when the others resigned?"

India checked her hair for split ends. "It's not that easy. I mean, we had processes to work through. Bryce and I were just looking after everything until we could get some nominations organized."

"Your partner was on the committee for a while, wasn't she?" Amanda asked.

India stubbed out her cigarette. "Pat didn't really have the time for Spectrum. She put in for a couple of months, but she wasn't that interested really. She only did it because I asked her to."

"I read her resignation." Amanda lifted a photocopy from her file. "She seemed concerned about Spectrum's management."

"It's not easy to run a voluntary organization,"

142

India said defensively. "Everyone has different goals. It's easy to criticize the people who are visible. Bryce worked really hard for Spectrum."

"It looks like a lot of people resigned after he became president," Mary said. "Any idea why?"

"It's always like that in voluntary organizations," India said. "People come and go, especially in summer. Energy moves." Tears welled suddenly. "I can't believe this. It's like a nightmare."

"What was Pat doing in New Zealand last week?" Amanda asked.

India stared, perplexed. "What are you talking about? Pat was in Sydney." Self-doubt seeped into her eyes. It was almost as if she expected to find herself mistaken.

"Where were you?" Mary asked.

"Here." India said. "Normally I go with her, on business trips. But I've been so tired lately."

"When did you hear about Bryce?"

"I read it in the papers. Saturday, I think." India leaned back in her chair, head to one side like a forlorn child. "I can't believe it."

"You were close to him?" Amanda asked.

India brushed a strand of hair from her eyes. "We were good friends. We worked together for two years."

"So how did you feel when he took off, leaving you to pay everything by yourself?" Mary interjected bluntly.

India's mouth trembled. "There's no proof that's what he intended. Anything could have happened. Maybe he was in some trouble..."

"I suppose you're hearing all about poor misunderstood Bryce," said a voice from the doorway,

143

and a sturdy dark-haired woman entered the room. Approaching India, she dropped a casual arm around her shoulders. "Sorry, honey. We'll just have to disagree on this one." Looking Amanda and Mary up and down, she said, "Mmm . . . the police improve their public image all the time. I'm Pat Degrassi, by the way."

Mary performed the introduction formalities, explaining that Amanda was in charge of the New Zealand investigation into Bryce Petty's death.

"I believe you were in Wellington last week," Amanda said.

Pat Degrassi looked unfazed. "That's right."

"You didn't tell me." India reproached her.

"You weren't in the mood to listen. Remember?"

"What was the reason for your trip?" Mary asked.

"Business."

"Could you be more specific?"

Pat smiled. "Someone attempted to rip off my partner. I went over to sort it out."

"You saw Bryce Petty?"

"I sure did." Supremely confident.

"We've impounded the rental car you were driving," Amanda said. "As we speak it's being taken apart by our forensic lab."

For a split second Pat looked startled, then she burst out laughing. "You think I killed that spineless jerk! You must be crazy."

"We have eye witnesses who saw your car at Mr. Petty's apartment the afternoon the crime was committed," Amanda said. "It's no laughing matter, Ms. Degrassi."

"Forgive me. But I think it is." Catching a horrified look from her girlfriend, Pat Degrassi said,

"Why should I pretend, for heaven's sake? The little shit got exactly what was coming to him."

Mary looked mildly incredulous. For a suspect, Pat Degrassi was either remarkably arrogant or remarkably innocent.

"What time were you at Mr. Petty's apartment?" Amanda asked.

Pat took an electronic organizer from her jacket. "Two thirty till three. I told him if he didn't hand that money over I'd break every bone in his body."

India was open-mouthed. "You said you got a loan."

"I did," Pat said coldly. "For your half."

"But —"

"You don't get it, do you?" she said. "We would have been up for the lot if your precious Bryce hadn't paid his share. So I got the money off him."

"How did you do that exactly?" Amanda asked.

"He wrote me a check. I cashed it and transferred the money to my account here," Pat said. "He'd already spent twenty grand."

"Which bank did you use?" Amanda asked.

"The ANZ. I can't remember the name of the street . . . the main drag."

"Lambton Quay?"

Pat nodded. "I went straight down there. Told him if he tried to cancel it I'd hunt him down and cut off his balls."

"I can't believe you did this," India whispered.

"What did you expect me to do?" Pat said harshly. "Stand around wringing my hands and making excuses for him like the rest of you?"

Amanda concentrated on her voice trying to match it with the one she'd heard on Bryce Petty's answer machine. Degrassi's accent seemed broader. "Did you phone Mr. Petty that day?"

"No. I just turned up. Boy, was he ever surprised."

"How did you find out where he lived?"

"I rang every gym in town." Pat grinned. "A guy with so little personality has to make up for it somehow."

"Did you take a gun with you?" Amanda asked.

Pat looked her straight in the eye. "If I'd wanted to kill that piece of shit, Inspector, I'd have done it with my bare hands."

"I take it that's a no," Mary said.

"I've never handled a gun in my life," Pat responded. "Now, if there's nothing else, I'd appreciate some time alone with my girlfriend."

"There's one more thing." Amanda got to her feet. "Would you mind showing me the clothing you were wearing that afternoon."

"I wish I could, but I just took everything to the cleaners." Pat felt around in her pockets, found a drycleaning chit and handed it to Amanda. "Black jacket and mushroom pants. I can't remember which shirt. They're all white."

"The money . . ." Mary inquired as Pat showed them out.

"I paid it to the court this morning," She released a soft whistle. "Thirty years of loan repayments for me and India. I think Bryce got off lightly, don't you?"

* * * * *

146

"You buy that?" Mary asked after a few minutes driving along the palm-lined St. Kilda Esplanade.

Amanda finished checking and rewinding the interview tape and sealed it in a labeled plastic bag. "Bryce Petty was obviously your classic chickenshit. I think he'd roll over for someone like Degrassi."

"The Niall woman seemed genuine enough. Pathetic, really. Can you believe she was still defending the schmuck?" Mary gave a long sigh. "I guess it pushes buttons for me. I was divorced a few years back. It's not easy to admit you've been living in denial about someone. All those friends saying I told you so. It's like ... if they're right, what sort of an idiot does that make you?"

So, she was straight. Amanda wondered if Mary had consciously wanted to let her know that. "Are you involved with anyone now?" she asked.

Mary shook her head. "It's lean pickings out there, if you're choosy. And frankly, after Jason, I'd rather be alone." It sounded like a well-rehearsed lie. "How about you?"

"I have someone," Amanda said. "Not full time. We're in separate cities."

"Long-distance love ... I guess it has its advantages."

Amanda tried to think of one. "It suits me," she said.

Mary wound through leafy groves where tall stone houses peeped from behind electrified walls. "This is Brighton," she said. "Very respectable. Some old money, lots of social climbers."

The Petty house was a modest dwelling compared

with its neighbor, a flamingo pink concrete mansion with marble lions guarding its fortified gates. "Mafia house," Mary commented. "Get the fountains."

They parked in the street and walked up the terra-cotta pathway to the Petty's front entrance. Next door a dog barked hysterically and an Italian-accented voice yelled *shaddup.* Amanda glanced at Mary, whose mouth twitched.

Mrs. Petty answered the door and took a startled step back when she recognized Amanda.

Identifying herself and apologizing for disturbing the household at such a difficult time, Mary said, "We'd just like a few words. May we come in?"

"Jim isn't here at the moment, I'm sorry." Mrs. Petty showed them into an immaculate drawing room dominated by a reproduction of the *Last Supper* hanging above the fireplace.

A hand-colored photograph of two young children, presumably Bryce and Glenys, graced the wall opposite. Majestic flower arrangements perched atop pedestals at either end of the room, waxen lilies at their centers. The air was scented with a powdery freshener.

Clearing her throat, Amanda said, "How was your flight?"

"The meal was very nice. You don't expect that on a plane." Mrs. Petty sat down on the edge of a cream velvet sofa and adjusted the linen arm cover.

"Your daughter Glenys told me you had a visitor from Spectrum a couple of weeks ago," Amanda said. "Who was that?"

Mrs. Petty moistened her lips. Behind her thick glasses, her eyes seemed to jitter from the floor to the ceiling. "I can't remember her name. She was looking for Bryce."

"Did you tell her where to find him?" Amanda asked.

"I didn't know where he was."

According to Patrick Ryan Mrs. Petty had known of Bryce's whereabouts soon after he vanished. Amanda glanced toward Mary, sensing she was also intrigued by the lie.

"Does the name Pat Degrassi sound familiar to you?" Mary asked.

"That was it," Mrs. Petty said. "She said she was a friend of the young lady who was in trouble with Bryce . . . India." Her voice seemed to bubble up from a deep well of tension. Amanda half expected her to giggle, but instead she got abruptly to her feet, her expression one of well-worn apology. "I'm sorry. Would you ladies like a cup of tea?"

"No. That's very kind of you," Mary said. "But we have a couple more questions."

Mrs. Petty sat down again, stretching her dress over plump stockinged knees. Her gaze wavered somewhere between Mary and Amanda.

"We were speaking to the private investigator you hired," Amanda said. "He said he gave you Bryce's address a month ago."

"Oh." Mrs. Petty adjusted a cushion.

"So you did know where he was when Pat Degrassi came to see you," Mary said. "Are you quite sure you didn't tell her?"

Mrs. Petty was adamant. "I didn't tell anyone. Not even Jim."

"Your husband was angry when he found out you'd hired Mr. Ryan, wasn't he?"

Mrs. Petty didn't answer.

"I'm puzzled about your husband," Amanda interjected softly. "Would you say he's normally a sensible man?"

Mrs. Petty's wiped her hands on her knees. Amanda felt like a brute, harassing a woman who had just lost her son.

"Jim does what he thinks is best," Mrs. Petty said.

"But you must have been shocked when he gave Bryce the money," Mary commented. "I know how I would have felt."

"He regretted it in the end." Mrs. Petty stared at the photograph of her children.

"I understand you were against lending Bryce the money at all," Amanda worked around the point. "Why was that?"

Mrs. Petty removed her glasses and rubbed her eyes. "We worked hard for this house. And with Jim sick . . . well, you don't know what's going to happen, do you. And it didn't seem fair, really, lending an amount like that to Bryce, when he'd done something wrong." She fidgeted with a button on her cardigan. "Glenys asked us for some help when she bought her house last year, but Jim refused. It's always been like that. Bryce was the favorite."

"Glenys must have felt bitter," Mary said.

Avoiding her gaze, Mrs. Petty studied an

elaborately painted enamel clock on a nearby china cabinet.

Recalling Jim Petty's dismissive remarks about his wife's attachment to the clock her son had taken, Amanda remarked, "That's an attractive piece. Is it very old?"

"It belonged to my grandmother." Mrs. Petty gave a small sigh. "We all got something when she died . . . us granddaughters. She remembered us specially."

"Your husband mentioned a clock Bryce took when he went to New Zealand. Was it that one?"

Color flooded Mrs. Petty's face. A muscle twitched beside her mouth. "Yes," she said in a thin uneven voice. "He had all that money and he took my clock."

"How did you get it back?"

"That's what I hired Mr. Ryan for," Mrs. Petty said, as if this were surely obvious.

"You asked him to get the clock back for you?"

"Not in so many words. I asked him to find Bryce, and he did."

"What then?" Amanda asked.

"I wrote and asked him to send my clock back. But he'd sold it. Then Jim found out about Mr. Ryan." Her eyes fastened on the door, as if expecting to see her husband appear at any moment. "Jim didn't care about the clock. He said Bryce would get it in the end, anyway . . . when we passed on. But I was keeping it for Glenys, you see. So I had to get it back."

Amanda's mind raced. "How did you do that?"

"There aren't that many antique dealers in

Wellington," Mrs. Petty said breezily. "I must have rung all of them." She got up and went over to the clock, extracting a slip of paper from beneath it. "I keep everything," she said and handed Amanda the receipt for her purchase.

"I want to talk about Pat Degrassi for a moment." Mary digressed. "Did you know she paid the damages to the court this morning?"

Mrs. Petty's attention seemed to wander. "I don't know about financial matters. Jim looks after everything."

"Did you know your son gave Ms. Degrassi a check on the day he was killed?"

Mrs. Petty stared. "I don't understand."

"Tell me about Ms. Degrassi's visit," Mary said. "What did you talk about with her?"

"I told you . . . she wanted to know where Bryce was."

"That's all?"

"I showed her my orchids. She was very interested." Mrs. Petty slid one of her feet a little way out of its shoe. Her leg was no longer bandaged, Amanda noticed. Beneath the opaque support hose her skin appeared bruised. "She seemed a nice girl."

Nice was not a word Amanda would have used to describe Pat Degrassi. "Did you tell your husband about her?" she asked.

"I didn't see any point."

"You seem to do rather a lot of things behind your husband's back," Mary remarked.

Mrs. Petty took this as criticism and responded

with a flash of anger. "It's my son's funeral tomorrow, and if you don't mind I've things to do." Abruptly, she lowered her eyes.

"There is one more thing," Amanda murmured. "About your daughter Glenys." She wondered if she imagined Mrs. Petty's faint start. "Do you know why she would have phoned Bryce on the day he was killed?"

Mrs. Petty was silent, her mouth compressed. Amanda was certain she could detect a trace of panic in her watery gaze. "She didn't say anything about that to me."

"Glenys normally tells you things?"

"We're mother and daughter."

"Remind me . . ." Amanda was niggled slightly by a slight discrepancy in the two women's accounts of Mrs. Petty's arrival in Tauranga. "When did your daughter collect you from Tauranga airport last Wednesday?"

Mrs. Petty blinked. "I think it was about half past six."

"That was when your flight left Rotorua," Amanda said. "So it must have been closer to seven, surely."

Mrs. Petty made a small gesture of distress. "Yes, I suppose it was. I'm sorry. It was such a terrible night, it's all muddled . . ."

Evasive answer. Attempting to fathom her thinking, Amanda said, "Glenys believes your husband may have given Bryce the money as a way of undermining you? Could that be true?"

Mrs. Petty lowered her head, the picture of weary defeat. "Jim is like that. He has to be right about things."

There was something else, Amanda thought. Beneath the dull resignation, houseproud Mrs. Petty sounded strangely triumphant.

CHAPTER FOURTEEN

Melbourne was renowned for rapid weather changes, the four seasons in one day. In keeping with this reputation, the sky had shifted from insipid blue to menacing gray during the time they were with Mrs. Petty. The daylight was fading and as they drove along the Esplanade, rain began to fall, painting the sea a dreary monochrome.

"You know what I think," Mary said. "I think she knows who killed him. It could be the Degrassi woman, it could be the husband, it could even be the daughter. But she knows."

"I think she suspects her husband," Amanda said. "She's hiding something. That's for sure."

"She's the kind of woman who derives her only power from knowing things," Mary mused. "She's a housewife in her fifties. Her kids have left home. She thinks her husband is carrying on with other women. Obviously it's an insecure situation. I'll bet she's spent her life getting dirt on him so she can keep him in line."

"In exchange for keeping her mouth shut, she gets respectability and a roof over her head?" Amanda knew the script from a hundred other cases. Marriage was built on trade-offs. Emotional, physical, financial. Find out where someone was cheating and you could often solve a crime. "You think she's stashed some evidence?"

"If he's the killer, I'd bet money on it. But it's too soon to rule out Degrassi."

"I want the pathology reports on that rental car before I interview her again," Amanda said.

"If she's telling the truth, Petty died between three-fifteen and five-thirty," Mary said. "So who's in the frame?"

"The guy who thought he heard shots was watching Ricki Lake," Amanda said. "The show runs from three-thirty to four-thirty, which means Degrassi could be telling the truth, and the killer could have arrived after she left. Of course our talk show junkie might have heard almost anything —"

"Mrs. Petty is our weak link," Mary said. "She'll serve her husband up on a plate before she'll go down with him. Trust me. She hates his guts."

She was probably right, Amanda reflected. No one

ever hated men as passionately as the women who had to live with them.

"Let's turn up the heat on her." Mary was speeding along her mental track. "You said the son saw Mr. Petty at a gay sauna. Maybe he's been booked. And there's the escort services. We can check his phone bills and his credit card charges . . ."

"That's a lot of time to commit." Amanda could visualize the return date on her air ticket receding into a nebulous future. "We could just lean on him, instead — try for a confession."

"Haven't you done that?"

"There's a limit, Mary. He has a strong alibi, we've been unable to put him at the scene and he's a grieving father."

"There's got to be a hole somewhere."

"I'd like to find it without squeezing facts to fit theories."

Mary shot her a sharp look. "Are you implying something about the way I work?"

Disconcerted, Amanda watched raindrops bouncing off the car bonnet. She was not used to working with a senior female detective who behaved as an equal, she realized with a flash of self-awareness. Mary Devine was bringing a fresh, questioning perspective to the investigation and Amanda was feeling defensive. "I'm sorry," she said.

"No worries." Mary cut through the St. Kilda shops onto tree-lined Barkly Street, mentioning she needed to drop by home. She parked outside a red brick bungalow and reached for a grocery bag in the back seat. "I have a few things to do. You're welcome to come in."

She cleared the mail and led Amanda around the house and up a concrete ramp to a side door. Inside, the place was warm and homely, with big soft armchairs and old fashioned drapes. Skylights in the kitchen and living area created a feeling of space that was usually absent from houses built during the Depression years. The walls were lined with tall bookcases and leafy houseplants. Opera played on the stereo.

"Sit down," Mary invited, methodically unpacking groceries. "Drink?"

Before Amanda could answer, a woman in an electric wheelchair swished into the room, greeting Mary with a contorted smile.

"Amanda, meet my sister Paula," Mary said.

"You're staying for dinner?" Paula asked, each word clearly a task.

"I wish we could," Mary said. "It's lousy weather out there now."

We're entitled to a meal break, Amanda thought, hoping Mary wasn't rushing for her sake.

"Amanda's over from New Zealand. We're working together on an investigation," Mary said as she arranged some bread around a bowl of what appeared to be ratatouille.

Paula cocked her head. "What part?"

"Wellington," Amanda said. "The capital city."

"We've been there," Mary remarked. "We went hitch-hiking around New Zealand after Paula graduated." She helped Paula position her chair at a table in the sunroom that adjoined the kitchen, then began feeding her.

Amanda felt completely at a loss, alternately embarrassed and dismayed. Paula appeared to have some terrible muscle-wasting condition. Her speech had been affected, so the disease was probably advanced.

"It was a great trip, wasn't it?" Mary reminisced as Paula chewed laboriously. "We even walked the Milford Track."

Paula slanted a look at her sister. "Heaven on earth."

"Apart from those biting sandflies . . . big as bloody dogs."

The kettle whistled.

"I'll get that," Amanda said, guiltily relieved to escape to the kitchen. Locating coffee grounds and a plunger, she called, "You want coffee, Paula?"

"She'll have herb tea." Mary entered and took a fragrant-smelling carton from the pantry. Responding to Amanda's unasked question, she said, "She's got multiple sclerosis and she had a stroke last year."

"She lives here with you all the time?"

Mary nodded. "I take a few days off when she's having a rough patch. They've been pretty good about it at work."

How do you have a life? Amanda wanted to ask. But thinking about Paula, trapped in a body that refused to function, she was silent.

They picked up Pat Degrassi's clothes from the dry cleaners and took them back to the station. They hadn't been cleaned, which was good news. They also hadn't been involved in the Petty murder.

"Either she wore something else or she left these folded up in another room while she killed him,"

Mary commented, tagging them for the lab. "I guess the bank video will help."

Amanda dialed the Wellington CIB and got through to the inquiry center. D.S. Solomon took the call. Austin Shaw was at the hospital visiting his mother, he said. Harrison was checking Petty's alibi once more. Bergman and Brody were interviewing a newspaper boy who saw someone near Petty's apartment building when he delivered the *Evening Post* that night.

"What time?"

"Around four."

Amanda felt a small flutter of excitement. "Can he give a description?"

"We're working on it," Solomon said. "He's one of those skittish type kids. Wants to see our guns, ride in a car..."

"How about the parents?"

"Both work at the university." Solomon's tone made it clear this was no recommendation. "They're worried about psychological damage."

"Tell them we'd really value their feedback on the interview process," Amanda said. "And take them in the car too. Blue lights... the works."

"Anything happening at your end?" Solomon asked.

Amanda told him about Pat Degrassi. Then she asked after his wife.

"They're both great," Solomon said. "Her and the baby."

"Congratulations."

"Ten pounds," he said. "She'll be a prop at that rate."

A prop was a rugby team position, Amanda assumed. "How did your daughter's match go?"

"Brilliant. Oughta be a prospect for the Junior All Blacks. But they don't take girls. Don't know where she's gonna play after next season." His tone was despondent.

"She sounds like a prospect for Police College," Amanda said.

"Yeah, there's always that." Solomon sighed. "She's a crack shot. Had her down at the pistol range last week. Knocked me off the board." There was a pause. "Tell me something, honestly. What's it like for a woman cop?"

What did he want to hear? That the world would treat his daughter fairly? "I don't suppose it's too much different from football," Amanda said. "To get a place on the team your daughter had to be better than the boys, right?"

Solomon was quiet.

"I've got a job for you," Amanda said. "Do you like antiques?"

Leo's Spaghetti Bar was a large noisy restaurant a few yards from St. Kilda's red light district. The food was cheap, the service disorganized, and the coffee extremely strong. Outside, a group of Jesus people were preaching to the junkies who frequented the sorry-looking park across the road. This annoyed a busker who sang Bob Dylan songs nearby, and he was telling everyone passing that the Lord never said anything against marijuana. Inside Leo's a vagrant had just made off with a takeout cappuccino without paying and the restaurant staff were shouting at one another in Italian.

On a wistful note, Carolyn said, "It won't be like this for much longer. They're cleaning up the neighborhood."

St. Kilda brought together a unique assortment of people, she explained. Traditionally a Jewish area, over the years its seaside charm had attracted a thriving counterculture of hippies, gays and writers. Gentrification had been a slow process, resisted by locals who cherished their suburb's character. But real estate developers had gradually moved in, tearing down lovely old homes on the seashore and replacing them with upmarket apartment buildings. To lure trendy young professionals into the area and inflate property values, they were now pressuring the police and City Council to get rid of the prostitutes, bag ladies and homeless. "It's not as if it's the crime capital of Melbourne," she grumbled. "What's a few curb crawlers, for God's sake?"

The waiter took their orders. Strangely, Amanda couldn't work up much of an appetite. Her mind strayed constantly to Mary Devine, feeding her sister, washing and changing her like a baby. Amanda had thought managing a permanent relationship would be tough. Imagine swapping places with Mary.

"You're miles away." Carolyn laughed. "You haven't heard a thing I was saying."

Amanda grimaced. "Tell me again."

"I was just saying I talked to my friend Chloe. Remember — the director who worked for Spectrum. She told me something very interesting." She topped up their wine. "A while back the cops raided a gay and lesbian nightclub here. They strip-searched everyone. Four hundred people."

"On what basis?" Amanda was stunned. She had assumed Australia was as liberal in its treatment of gays as New Zealand.

"It was a complete scandal," Carolyn said. "The cops came up with some excuse about drugs, but everyone thinks it was some kind of mates deal with the Tasmanians."

"I don't get it."

"The Tasty raid was payback," Carolyn said. Gays and lesbians in Melbourne had led a national boycott of Tasmanian produce to protest the outlawing of homosexuality in that conservative state. Two gay men had taken a human rights complaint to the United Nations and won. Australian federal law made discrimination illegal, but the Tasmanians refused to bring their state legislation in line with this, so gays and lesbians had taken action. "Now the police are in deep shit for doing favors for their Tassie mates," Carolyn said. "There's a class action pending. Obviously evidence is an issue."

"Four hundred statements is probably a good start," Amanda remarked.

"That's where it gets really interesting. Chloe was there filming someone's birthday party for her current affairs show. It's the only live footage of the raid. She stashed the tape in a speaker before the cops took the camera, then came back for it the next day. As you can imagine, we're talking about a hot property."

Amanda considered the issues. No doubt the tape revealed the faces of patrons who might not want to be seen at a gay nightclub. On the other hand it

163

showed the police conducting a raid that was now the subject of a lawsuit.

"Spectrum was ecstatic," Carolyn said. "As soon as the networks heard about the tape they were offering all sorts of money. Then wham . . . it vanishes."

"Why am I surprised?" Amanda said dryly. "Don't tell me, your friend handed it over to Bryce Petty . . ."

Carolyn smiled. "Mind like a razor."

"Where is it now?"

"That's what everyone would like to know. Chloe has her theories . . . she thinks Bryce might have sold it to the cops."

"You're joking." As if the police weren't in enough trouble without perverting the course of justice. Amanda sprinkled Parmesan cheese on the steaming pasta the waiter set down in front of her. "I can't believe the police would have bought that tape," she said, after a couple of mouthfuls. "For a start, the decision would have to come right from the top."

Carolyn shrugged. "That's how corruption works in this town."

Amanda wound spaghetti onto her fork. What if the police hadn't paid for the tape but they'd sent someone to retrieve it? She'd joked about a professional hit. Maybe her flippant comment would come back to haunt her. "I'll check it out," she said.

"Be careful." Carolyn chewed thoughtfully on a prawn. "New Zealand might be a squeaky clean little place, but it's not the same here. This country was built on graft and corruption. No one wants to admit it, but it's part of the national psyche."

164

Amanda had read about the horrors of life in the early penal colonies of Australia. After the United States had refused to accept any more convict transports from the English, they had set up Australia up as a gulag to absorb the vast overflow from their foundering penal system. Used as slave labor, transported convicts were subjected to systematic starvation, torture and floggings, their despotic captors given free reign by a disinterested colonial administration.

Carolyn, an enthusiastic social historian, insisted that the behaviors and attitudes entrenched in modern Australia were a legacy of its sordid past. "Take misogyny," she declared over their dessert. "The only reason women were transported here was to curb homosexuality. They were literally turned into a class of sexual slaves . . . purchased like sides of beef, straight off the convict ships. There were only two ways a woman was registered as a citizen here — 'married' or 'concubine.' Incredible, isn't it?"

An image of Mrs. Petty sprang into Amanda's mind. Passive in the face of her husband's contemptuous disregard, was she a second-class citizen in her own mind as well as his? Attitudes didn't vanish overnight. She thought about Glenys Petty's comment, *I'm not going to turn out like her.* How many generations had it taken?

"Australia has changed a lot since I was a girl," Carolyn said. "At least, women have changed. It's like a breath of fresh air. Our expectations are so much higher than our mothers'. Quite frankly I think men are in a state of shock. I mean, they're not allowed to hang their wives for disobedience anymore . . ."

"So, what are they doing instead?"

"Beer, football and wife-beating, usually in that order," Caroline replied cynically. "A bloke can still find docile handmaidens to pat his ego and cover his ass, of course. Hell, I do it myself. There I am in a meeting, and some wonderboy is spouting the most cretinous garbage, and I'm sitting there smiling and nodding like I'm impressed..." She put her glass down. "Does that happen to you?"

"I used to take some shit from the guys back home," Amanda said. "But it's been easier in New Zealand." She thought about the people she worked with. Sexism certainly existed, especially among the top brass, and she was well aware tokenism had played a role in her fast-track career. "I still get asked to give the 'feminine perspective' on a case —"

"Women thinking with one mind the way we do . . ."

"And there's our natural instinct for fashion," Amanda said, mock-serious. "They were thinking about changes to the female uniform a few months back, so guess who they asked."

"No!" Carolyn snorted. "I hope you said tight leather pants, soft black shirt, Sam Browne belt . . ."

"Actually I said miniskirts would be fetching."

"You didn't?"

"A sergeant from Uniform Branch came and lectured me on how sexist my concept was."

"She didn't get the joke?"

"He," Amanda corrected. "It was a man."

Carolyn rolled her eyes. "Only in New Zealand."

CHAPTER FIFTEEN

Amanda peered at the digital clock next to her bed. It was 5:00 a.m. Too early for phone calls. "Do you have any idea what time it is?" she demanded.

There was a pregnant silence at the other end, then Harrison said, "Isn't it seven o'clock in Melbourne?"

Amanda groaned. "It's five in the morning. We're two hours *behind* New Zealand, remember."

Carolyn stuck her head around the door, eyes heavy with sleep. Stifling a yawn, she said, "Since I'm up I thought I'd make coffee. Want some?"

Mouthing a grateful *yes, please,* Amanda said into the phone, "This had better be good."

"It is," Harrison said.

Amanda elbowed herself into a more comfortable position. "You got something on the car?"

"So far it looks clean, but Professor McDougall is taking it apart just like you said. The hotel room was clean too, but we just blew Mr. Petty's alibi wide open." Harrison grew breathless. "He left the hotel at quarter to three and got a cab to the diocese. He was there till four, not four-thirty, like he claimed. The Bishop's secretary recorded it and now the Bishop and some other church guys have given sworn statements to that effect. He said he went to the museum afterwards but there's no sign of him on the security film."

"So we can't account for him between four and five-thirty?" Amanda felt relief wash over her. Caught out on a lie. They'd have a search warrant for the Petty house before midday. What time was the funeral? she wondered. Maybe they could do the place while the Pettys were at the cemetery. That would certainly turn the heat up.

"There's something else." Harrison's voice thinned a little. "It's Anya and Sara. They got a brick through their front window. Anya says it's some mates of Mel's."

"Do we have names?"

"No."

"I'll talk to D.S. Gibbs," Amanda said. "We'll see what Mel has to say about it."

"There's more," Harrison said. "Some women are meant to be coming round to see Sara later today. They want her to drop the complaint."

"What?"

"They told Anya they're going to have a meeting with Mel and Jolene and decide how they should be punished. They think everything should be kept within the community."

Amanda's brain sluggishly refused to process the information. "Are you telling me a bunch of nosy parkers are going to hold some kind of people's court to pass judgment on Mel and Jolene? What are we talking about here — a ban from the women's dances or maybe the feminist bookstore refuses to sell *Deneuve* to them?"

"Anya doesn't know what to do."

She could start by getting a spine, Amanda felt like saying. Sara would almost certainly buckle under pressure and withdraw her complaint. She reached for her diary and located Roseanne's phone number. "We're going to arrange a small vacation for Sara," she informed Harrison. "You go talk to that girlfriend of yours. I want the names of every woman involved in this."

Harrison made a small strangled noise. "What are you going to do?"

"Whatever I have to," Amanda said coldly. Telling Harrison to expect her back in town some time in the next two days, she hung up and followed the smell of coffee beans into the kitchen.

"Everything okay?" Carolyn set two huge mugs on the table.

"I hope so," Amanda said. "Sorry you got woken."

"Don't worry about it. I could use an extra hour in the office before I go to court."

"The divorce from hell?"

"Almost as bad — a custody hearing." Carolyn

pulled a face. "There's hardly a day goes by that I don't thank the Goddess that Sally and I didn't have kids."

Amanda tried to picture herself with a baby in a pushchair. The image that immediately sprang to mind was one of Madam in her cat carrier, yowling all the way to the vet's surgery for her biannual checkup. "I know exactly what you mean," she said.

"It's not that we never thought about it," Carolyn said. "I mean, you do, don't you, with all that biology happening every month?"

Amanda made a noncommittal sound. She had sometimes watched Debby cooing over animals at the zoo and imagined her with a baby.

"You get to a certain age and you just have to decide," Carolyn said. "And you live with that decision for the rest of your life."

There was a flatness in her voice that made Amanda look up sharply. "It's still not too late, you know."

Carolyn's expression became remote. "It is for me. I had my womb removed last year."

"There's been a development." Mary shoved her handbag into the bottom drawer of her desk. "I've got Lou Riddell downstairs. She's confessed."

Amanda felt her jaw drop. "You're kidding."

"She was picked up in Commercial Road last night, drunk and disorderly." Mary gathered up her notebook. "Apparently she spilled her guts to the arresting officer. No doubt she'll be telling a different story this morning."

"She's a head case," Amanda said. "I've just spoken to Wellington. Jim Petty gave a false alibi."

Mary looked up sharply. "Really?"

"I want a search warrant."

"It'll take an hour or so." Mary glanced at the clock on the wall. "It's the funeral later this morning."

"Is that a problem?"

"It could be, if we don't find anything." The media had them under a microscope, she explained wearily. In recent times the police had shot dead a record number of people and their methods were coming in for some flak. Channel Ten would be thrilled to film outraged mourners wringing their hands while a bunch of detectives tore the Petty house apart.

Amanda gave an impatient shrug. "We'll just have to take our chances."

"I'll get the paperwork underway." Mary sounded resigned. "Why don't you start on Lou. I think she'll respond to some softening up."

Amanda could hardly wait.

Neither, it seemed, could Lou Riddell.

"I would have fixed my hair," she informed Amanda huffily, "if your staff had seen fit to provide me with a mirror." She glowered at the impassive constable locking the door.

"I understand you've got something to tell us," Amanda said.

Lou clasped a theatrical hand to her pointed

breasts and announced, "I did it. I killed Bryce Petty."

"No you didn't," Amanda said mildly.

Lou stared at her. "I did. I shot him."

"Where's the gun?"

With a dismissive sniff, Lou said, "I got rid of it, of course. God only knows where is it now."

"You're wasting my time," Amanda said. "You weren't even in New Zealand —"

"I was! I can show you my passport." Lou cast an accusing look at the constable. "If it's still in my handbag."

"So, where did you dump the gun?" Amanda repeated.

"In a rubbish bin. I don't remember where exactly . . ."

"Think!"

Lou produced an aggrieved simper, "I'm trying, Inspector. I want to help." She tapped her carefully manicured nails on the table. "I was in such a state, I can hardly remember a thing."

"Tell me about the shooting."

"I can't. I've blocked it out of my mind. The blood . . ." She fanned herself wanly, the star of her own badly scripted soap opera. "I did it. Isn't that enough for you?"

The confession was patently bogus. Disproving it would not be difficult, Amanda felt certain. But it would waste valuable time. Irritated, she said, "Do you have any idea the penalties for making a false statement?"

"Of course I do," Lou replied with affronted dignity.

"Then why are you here?" Amanda asked. "You've

172

got three previous convictions. Do you want to go back inside?"

Lou tilted her chin, her expression superior. "I feel sorry for you, Inspector. It must be hard to feel like a real woman doing a job like this."

Amanda took a deep breath. "I was asking you why you're confessing to crime you didn't commit, Lou. Is it attention you want, or have you got a boyfriend inside?"

Lou adopted a slow patronizing drawl. "As it happens, I'm not interested in men, Inspector."

Amanda wondered how she was supposed to respond to this revelation.

Lou continued. "I had forty-seven years of agony trapped in a man's body." Her eyes glittered with the martyred relish of a woman telling her childbirth story. "But that's behind me now. I'm a lesbian and proud of it."

She'd heard enough, Amanda thought. "You're free to go," she said matter-of-factly.

"You can't do that!" Lou was outraged. "I've turned myself in."

"We don't want you." Amanda hoped Mary would agree with her strategy. If Lou had anything to do with the killing she would now have to provide some concrete proof or return to the anonymity she so clearly resented.

"You stupid, incompetent bitch!" she hissed at Amanda. "I want to speak to your superiors right now. Is this what I'm paying my taxes for? So that some slut with a badge can treat me like this. I'll have you sacked. I'll —"

The testosterone suppressants hadn't quite taken, Amanda surmised. She stuck her notebook in her pocket and walked away as the tirade continued. "Get her out of here," she told the constable, "before I forget she's a lady."

Mary was on the phone when Amanda got upstairs. "I've told them to lock Riddell up," she said.

Amanda shifted a pile of reports off her chair so she could sit down. Her desk was a sea of papers. A Styrofoam cup was on its side, the remains of a takeout espresso soaking the papers nearby. "Why hold her? She doesn't know anything."

"It looks like progress. And she was in New Zealand last week."

"So was your national rugby team, but we're not interviewing them." Amanda mopped at the coffee residue with a Kleenex.

"She pissed you off, huh?" Mary said.

"Understatement." Amanda tossed the tissue in the trash. "We've got a break in this case, and I want a result. I don't have time to waste on attention-seekers like Riddell."

Mary plonked a document in front of her. "How does four men and a search warrant sound?"

"Like music to my ears." Amanda put on her coat. "If we haul ass maybe we can get done before the wake."

CHAPTER SIXTEEN

It took four hours to search the Petty home. They could have stopped after three, if they'd known about Jim Petty's heart attack. Only they didn't get the call until they were outside digging up the grounds.

"He was D.O.A.," Mary said. "Collapsed at the cemetery. They kept him alive twenty minutes or so. He died in the ambulance."

It was tacky to ask, but Amanda couldn't help herself. She'd been planning her final interview with him all morning. "Did he confess?"

"Someone at the cemetery thought he said

something about Bryce, but who knows?" Mary watched as members of their team loaded boxes of evidence into the police van parked in the Petty's driveway. "I guess it's a technicality at this point."

They had located several incriminating pieces of evidence. A blood-stained towel sealed in a plastic bag was stuffed in the aircon vent in the guest bedroom. A handful of bullets similar to those used by the killer were inside a sock in the bottom of Jim Petty's wardrobe, and a photograph of Bryce, which appeared to belong to the sequence found in his apartment, was tucked inside a gardening book next to Petty's bed.

"You were right," Amanda said. "It looks like Mrs. Petty stashed the towel somewhere he wouldn't find it. Everything else was more or less lying around."

"It's all pretty circumstantial." Mary's shoulders sagged with anticlimax. "I wish we'd found the clothing he was wearing."

They'd taken virtually the entire contents of his wardrobe. Every garment looked spotless. "We might get a trace match," Amanda said, conscious of a sense of futility. With their quarry lying in the morgue, there hardly seemed any point building an elaborate case against him. The evidence would now end up presented to a coronial inquest. Listlessly, she paced the fenceline with Mary, looking for signs of disturbed earth.

"I'd like to find that gun," Mary said.

"I'm sure Mrs. Petty will give us a full statement," Amanda said. "She won't want to be charged with accessory."

"Will you charge her at all?"

"She concealed evidence," Amanda said. "But they're not going to lock her up. Suspended sentence . . . that's my guess."

Mary's hair was curling in the fine drizzle. Her skin glowed with cold. She smiled at Amanda. "I've enjoyed working with you."

"Me too," Amanda said, again conscious of a welling attraction. Life was full of ifs and buts, she thought. If they weren't colleagues, she might have stroked away the damp hair clinging to Mary's forehead and kissed her.

"When will you go back?" Mary asked.

"Tomorrow, I hope."

They reached the cramped little hothouse where Mrs. Petty kept her precious orchids.

"I'll finish up in here," Amanda offered. "I think two would be kind of crowded."

Hunched inside the doorway, she watched Mary walk toward the van, her mobile to her ear. The sky rumbled, storm clouds breaking overhead. Rain began to pound on the glass roof. The place smelled green and damp. Ripe foliage brushed Amanda's cheeks as she moved along the shelves, lifting the heavy clay pots and poking her fingers into the wood chips around each plant.

It struck her as somehow incongruous that Mrs. Petty collected orchids. She gazed at a sensuous bloom, intrigued by its perfection. A chocolate-colored slipper adorned with freckles of green, its waxen petals extended like craving arms from its fleshy base. You simply couldn't make assumptions about people, she decided, lifting the exotic bloom and peeping into its tray.

A brass key gleamed at her. Amanda picked it up

and returned the orchid. It didn't matter how many pamphlets the police published, people would never learn. They still left their spare keys under potted plants.

A detective knocked at the door and said they were ready to go. With a final sweeping glance around the floor and walls, Amanda went out into the rain where he was waiting with an umbrella. Huddling beneath it, they ran for the cover of the Petty's back veranda.

"Have you locked up?" Amanda automatically tried the key she'd found and was mildly surprised when it didn't fit in the back door lock.

Puffing from his brief exertion, the hefty detective nodded. "I hear your perp's dropped dead on you, inconsiderate bastard." He peered up at the dark sky. "Shall we make a run for the van?"

"You go," Amanda said. "I won't be long."

She jogged around to the front entrance and inserted the key in the lock. Again it wouldn't budge. It was far too new to belong to some previous dwelling, she thought as she stared down at the tooling marks still apparent on its shaft. Puzzled, she bagged it and slipped it into her breast pocket. It was something else she would ask Mrs. Petty to explain.

The task of double-checking each piece of evidence against the inventory made at the search location normally fell to a junior detective. But Amanda figured it would be diplomatic to complete the job herself. She was surprised to be interrupted half way through by a constable who said there was a woman wanting to see her.

The waiting room was full of tabletop dancers waiting for a friend to be released. Pat Degrassi looked out of place among the thin, heavily made up women, but she seemed to be enjoying herself anyway. The center of attention, she was demonstrating a karate hold as Amanda approached. With an engaging grin, she said, "Just showing the ladies what to do if the punters give them any trouble."

"You could also call the police," Amanda suggested.

Peels of laughter erupted. "They'll be in the audience, love," a red-haired woman said. "Worst of the lot, if you ask me."

A couple of her companions handed Pat Degrassi their cards saying they did private functions for ladies like her. One of them was running a special on her snake act. Two for the price of one.

"You wanted to see me?" Amanda said.

Fending off more explicit invitations from the snake dancer, Pat Degrassi followed Amanda to an interview room. "Half of them are gay," she said, as if she needed to explain.

"I come from New York," Amanda told her. "I don't shock easily."

"What are you doing Down Under?"

"Investigating murders," Amanda sat down. "You know Bryce Petty's father died this morning?"

"India was there," Pat said. "It's the kind of thing you see on a telemovie, isn't it? They lower the coffin and someone keels over."

"What did you want to see me about?"

"Everything I told you yesterday was the truth," she said. "Except there's something I didn't tell you. With India there, I —"

"Whatever you say here is confidential," Amanda reminded her.

"It's okay. I've talked to her now." Pat slid her fingers back through her hair. "I don't know where to begin — the money, I guess. India and I were going to sell our house. But in the end we didn't have to. When Bryce scarpered he took something that belonged to Spectrum, you see. It was worth a lot of money . . . a videotape —"

"The raid on that gay bar?"

"You know about it?" Pat was surprised.

"I know that it disappeared."

"Look." Pat lowered her voice. "I didn't want to talk to the cops here . . . you understand?"

"You have the tape?"

"Not anymore. I sold it to Channel Nine and *voilà* . . . India and I get to keep the house."

"So, Bryce gave you the tape?"

"I was getting to that." Pat toyed absently with her pinky ring. "You're not going to believe this, but it just turned up in my letterbox last Saturday. I figured if you heard Bryce had it, then you saw it on TV, you'd start asking questions, and . . . Things look bad enough for me, right? I was there the day he got killed. I guess I had a motive . . ."

Amanda was silent. Pat saw herself as a prime suspect and was therefore anxious to prove her innocence. Amanda wondered what else she was holding onto. "Do you have any idea who put the tape in your letterbox?" she asked.

"I got pretty paranoid at first," Pat said. "I

thought I was being set up. But then I got to thinking. It's worth a lot of money. Why would anyone give it away?"

"There was nothing with it? A note . . ."

Pat shook her head. "It was wrapped up in brown paper with string around it. No name. Nothing. Hell, I'm not complaining. We were right in the shit till it showed up."

"Let's go back to the day you visited Bryce," Amanda said. "Where did you park?"

"In the visitors' spaces. Round the front by that wall."

Amanda mentally pictured the surroundings. A concrete wall separated Petty's apartment block from a bush area that traversed a gully. The search team had found the usual assortment of old combs, broken glass and cigarette butts in the vicinity, and a spot near the wall showed signs of trampling. But inquiries around the neighborhood had revealed it was the place local twelve-year-olds went to smoke cigarettes and read dirty magazines.

"Did you see any people in the area while you were there?" Amanda asked.

Pat shook her head. "It was amazingly quiet. Just some guy walking his dog."

Eventually they would piece together how Petty had done it, Amanda supposed. On a measured impulse, she said, "Well, you'll probably be glad to know we're expecting to close the investigation shortly. I just have a few loose ends to tidy up, then —"

"You mean you've got the person who did it?" Pat's expression hovered between curiosity and chagrin. "Why didn't you tell me?"

Amanda smiled inwardly. "I was interested in what you had to say."

"Yeah, I'll bet." Silent for a moment, Pat drummed her fingers on the table, then she said, "About the tape . . . I know it wasn't exactly mine to sell. I thought about handing it over to the liquidators, but I figured they'd use it to pay off Spectrum's debts and we'd still be stuck paying for the lawsuit. Then maybe Spectrum would get going again and all the same people would come back, acting like nothing ever happened. And the whole rotten cycle would start all over." She looked up. "You know what really stuns me? They could have stopped Bryce from wrecking that organization, but they just stood there watching. Worse than that, they stonewalled anyone who tried to blow the whistle."

"Misplaced loyalty," Amanda commented. "It's a fact of human nature."

Pat shook her head. "It was more than that. It was complicity."

"India was one of them."

"I know. And she's ended up paying for her share of the blame and everyone else's," Pat said bitterly.

"She was genuinely fond of Bryce, wasn't she?"

"Totally sucked in. She only wanted to see his good side." Pat frowned. "I had his number the minute I laid eyes on him, and he knew it. So he got the knives out right away . . . your classic wolf in sheep's clothing. Mr. Charming."

"They make the world's most successful criminals," Amanda noted. "Con men, serial killers, child molesters . . ."

"Football stars who butcher their ex-wives." Pat

182

stood up and buttoned her jacket. "They do okay in politics, too."

A few hours later, Amanda sat drinking coffee on Carolyn's sofa. Pat Degrassi's comments about complicity lingered in her mind and she got to thinking about the Sara Hart case.

Sara was now staying in Amanda and Roseanne's beach cottage to avoid a group of women who wanted her to comply with her own rape by remaining silent about it. The same patterning occurred in numerous incest, sexual harassment and domestic violence cases, where the victim was coerced or emotionally black-mailed into participating in a cover-up.

In every case, a complex equation was at work. The perpetrator needed silence so he could continue the offending he enjoyed. The individuals who saw what was happening but said nothing also had an investment in covering up. For they had behaved like cowards and wanted to avoid taking responsibility for the consequences. The equation continued into society, where denial of the problem went hand in hand with blaming the victim, absolving everyone from doing anything about it.

It stemmed from an investment in pretty pictures, she supposed. The happy marriage, the worthy com-munity organization, the lesbian utopia . . . Was that why Sara had to be silent? Was "keeping it in the community" a euphemism for keeping up pretenses?

In her mind's eye, Amanda saw Mrs. Petty again, limping behind her husband. What was her life about? Who was she inside the social fiction she propped up — a slipper orchid in a nondescript pod?

Amanda thought about herself and quite suddenly her life seemed as much an eggshell world as Mrs. Petty's, created so she could feel she belonged somewhere. Sadness swept over her. What was the point in it all?

Morosely, she turned on the television. It was the late news. A reporter was trying to make some sense out of the latest crisis in Bosnia. Amanda flicked across a few channels and found a movie. It was *Police Academy*. She felt so bad, she watched it for ten minutes. Then she turned it off and confronted the paperwork she had been avoiding. She had a report to write.

CHAPTER SEVENTEEN

Glenys Petty insisted on remaining with her mother while she gave her statement to Amanda. "She's told me everything," she said. "She was frightened of Dad or she would have come forward at the start."

"When did you know what had happened?" Amanda said, recalling Glenys's earlier insistence that her father had not killed Bryce.

Glenys slid a graceful hand beneath her hair, lifting it from her neck. "I only knew for sure after I arrived for the funeral." She offered a brief appeasing smile. "I was planning to talk with you."

"I'm sure," Amanda said, thinking *bullshit*.

"Please go easy on her," she pleaded at the door of the interview room. "She knows she's done wrong."

"I already went easy on your mother," Amanda said. She might have reached a few smart conclusions a little sooner, if she hadn't.

Mrs. Petty's nose was bright red from weeping. Clutching a saturated linen handkerchief, she could hardly lift her swollen eyes from the table.

Amanda briskly went through the formalities, then said, "I'm sure you don't want to be here any longer than necessary, Mrs. Petty. So I suggest you answer my questions fully and honestly. Do you understand?"

Mary Devine entered with a tray of evidence and laid several plastic bags on the table, their contents plainly visible.

"I'm holding a blood-stained towel." Amanda selected the most incriminating item. "Have you see this before, Mrs. Petty?"

"Yes. I found it among my husband's possessions when I unpacked his bag."

"Was it the only blood-stained item?"

"No." Mrs. Petty shifted her gaze to the barren wall opposite. "I got rid of everything else."

"What was there?"

"His shirt and pants, a tie . . . some other towels."

"Did your husband ask you to unpack for him?"

"I always did that," Mrs. Petty said. "Packing and unpacking."

"So you packed your husband's gun when you left for Wellington last week?"

Mrs. Petty was very still. "No."

"Are you saying he took it on the airplane with him?"

"He must have packed it himself," Mrs. Petty said. "I didn't see it."

"But you knew your husband owned a gun?"

"No."

Amanda could sense Glenys's hostility. You haven't seen anything yet, she thought. Over the past twelve hours she'd had plenty of time to consider the mishmash of evidence against Jim Petty. There were far too many unanswered questions and gaps in logic to declare the case closed.

"I found something among your household papers," Amanda fossicked among the evidence and retrieved a small pink slip in its sealed plastic envelope. "Do you recognize this?"

Mrs. Petty peered at it. "That's the docket for my clock."

"Look again," Amanda invited. "I have the receipt for your purchase of the clock elsewhere. This is the receipt the dealer issued when Bryce sold the clock to him."

"Oh . . . er, yes." Mrs. Petty said. "I believe it was with the clock. Bryce must have put it there."

Amanda heard Glenys's faint intake of breath.

"That's impossible." Mentally thanking Detective Solomon, Amanda referred to her notes. "Your son left your clock with the dealer to be valued. The dealer talked with his partners then made an offer over the phone the next day. Bryce accepted and the dealer posted him a check with this receipt for the goods. So Bryce could not have put it in the clock . . . he didn't have it anymore."

Mrs. Petty blinked. "It must have been Jim, then."

"Where did Jim get it?"

"From Bryce's apartment, I suppose." Mrs. Petty's response was snappish. She fiddled jerkily with the buttoned collar of her unflattering woollen frock.

"When did you first contact the dealer who had your clock?" Amanda asked.

"It must have been the day we saw you. The day after Bryce was . . ." Mrs. Petty shifted in her seat. "I phoned him in the morning, before your officer came to pick us up."

"You said in our discussion two days ago that you telephoned all the dealers in Wellington. We've been unable to trace such calls either from your hotel room or from Glenys's number." She watched color ebb and flow from Mrs. Petty's face. "Why did you lie about that?"

Mrs. Petty was silent.

Intercepting a darting look of panic from Glenys, Amanda held the pink slip up again. "You obtained the dealer's name from this receipt, didn't you? You've just told me your husband took it from Bryce's apartment. That means you must have known he killed your son the moment you saw it."

"No —" Mrs. Petty began.

"Yes. And then you concealed what your husband had done. Do you know what that means? That means I can have you charged with being an accessory."

Mrs. Petty blew her nose. Mouth trembling, she said, "I'm sorry —"

"I don't want your apologies," Amanda said. "I want to know where you dumped your husband's

188

clothing and the gun. I don't believe he carried all that incriminating evidence back here to Melbourne in his luggage."

Mrs. Petty cried softly against her arm. "He did. I told you. I got rid of it. I drove around and put it in rubbish bins."

"What about the suitcase?"

"I gave it to the St. Vincent de Paul mission."

"And the gun?"

Mrs. Petty flicked a sideways glance at her daughter. "I never saw it. Jim must have got rid of it."

"He didn't tell you?"

"We never talked about it."

"So the morning after your son was killed, you flew to Wellington, phoned the antique dealer who had your clock, then came downtown and lied to me. Afterwards you bought your clock from the dealer, and he felt so sorry for you he let you have it for the same amount he'd paid your son." Amanda poured herself a glass of water. "Why did your husband kill Bryce, Mrs. Petty?"

"Because of the money." Her voice wavered.

"So, even though your husband was not in any hurry to track Bryce down to get this money back, he was angry enough to kill him over it?"

Mrs. Petty said. "He lost his temper."

"You're saying he took the gun around there to threaten Bryce and when he found out about Ms. Degrassi, he shot your son? Then, instead of escaping as fast as he could, he hunted everywhere for information about your clock . . . the clock you said he couldn't give a damn about?"

"I don't know," Mrs. Petty said in a whisper.

"Can you explain how it is he left no bloody fingerprints anywhere?" Amanda demanded. "He opened drawers and cupboards and poked around in papers and hey, not a mark!"

Mrs. Petty undid her top button and eased her collar back. Her eyes were glazed.

"I think you're lying." Amanda placed a fax on the table in front of her. "This is a photocopy of your son's front door key." The document showed side, flat and profile views. Beside it she laid the key she had bagged during the search. "And this is a key I found in your orchid house yesterday morning. Would you like to compare them?"

Glenys seemed transfixed.

"How do you explain this, Mrs. Petty?"

"Jim asked me to get rid of it . . ."

"But you didn't. Why?"

"I don't know." She threaded her handkerchief through her watch strap.

"I think this was your key." Amanda said. "I think your husband didn't even know you had it. As soon as you got to Wellington, you visited your son's apartment and hunted for that receipt. He was away on Monday, wasn't he?"

Mrs. Petty knotted her hands together. When she lifted her head, it was to look at her daughter.

Glenys was as pale as the pearls at her throat, her gaze pained and questioning.

In a faltering voice, Mrs. Petty said, "I did go there. On Monday."

"And what did you find?"

"Bryce's gun," Mrs. Petty said. "And a video. I

thought it might be the program that caused all the trouble, so I took it. I was curious."

"And the docket for your clock?"

Mrs. Petty gave her daughter a look which oscillated somewhere between relief and despair. "I couldn't find anything about the clock. So I had to go back."

"When did you do that?"

"On Wednesday. I bought a ticket for a day trip to Rotorua and I gave it to another lady who was staying at the motel. I caught a plane to Wellington. It was really easy. I made up a name and bought the ticket with cash I got off my credit card at the bank . . ."

"And when you got to Wellington?"

"I put my bags in the left luggage and caught the bus downtown. I bought some new clothes and changed into them at the public conveniences."

"You were carrying the gun?"

"In my handbag." Mrs. Petty avoided her daughter's fixated stare. "It was heavy."

"What then?"

"I went to his apartment."

"What time was that?"

"About quarter past two."

"How did you get there?"

"I caught a taxi to that street that runs along the opposite side of the bush."

Which you then crossed. Amanda pictured Mrs. Petty squatting in the depression by the wall, watching her son's apartment, the most unlikely of assassins.

"I walked over to the other side and just as I was coming up to the wall, I heard a car. It's a small world, isn't it?" She almost smiled. "It was Pat Degrassi. I watched her . . . just like a spy." She might have been recounting a wholesome girls' adventure story, with herself as the heroine.

Amanda met Mary's eyes. She looked numb.

"I waited till she left," Mrs. Petty said. "Then I climbed over the fence and . . ." She released a long sigh. "I didn't want to kill him."

"What happened?" Amanda asked.

"He came to the door. He was in a state. He said something about ringing his bank. I pointed the gun at him and told him I wanted to know where my clock was. He said some rude things, but in the end he looked in his wallet and the docket was there."

"Did he attack you?" Amanda asked. Surely Petty would have tried to disarm his mother.

"Oh no. He just told me not to do anything stupid."

Amanda could imagine Bryce Petty concluding that his mother would never hurt him, that she would put the gun down and leave quietly. "What made you shoot him?" she asked.

She blinked and removed her glasses. "I said Jim and I were upset. He just started laughing. He said they had a plan — him and his father. First they would get the mortgage. Then Jim was going to take out a loan against his pension fund and withdraw everything out of the bank. Then he was going to leave me. Bryce was supposed to look after all the money. That way, when Jim died, there'd be nothing for me or Glenys." She wiped her eyes with the back of her hand. "He said it was his brilliant idea." She

192

turned to her daughter, her expression pleading. "I did it for you, darling. You were such a good girl and I never stood up for you once. All those years I let you down."

By some unspoken consensus, Amanda and Mary exited the room, leaving mother and daughter alone together.

"She shouldn't have confessed," Mary said in the corridor outside. "She could have gotten away with it."

Amanda glanced at the locked door. "But then Glenys would never have known."

"That her Mom finally stood up for her?" Mary sighed. "Better late than never, I suppose."

It took three and a half hours to fly back to Wellington the next day. Amanda sat beside a guy with a gas problem. Across the aisle two small children whined continuously. Crossing the Tasman Sea the plane hit turbulence and the seatbelt warning sounded.

"Makes you nervous doesn't it?" said the guy next door.

Speak for yourself, Amanda thought. "It's not so different from a car."

"Except you're in a big tin can thirty thousand feet up in the air." He released a shrill laugh which ended in a hiccup. "Sorry," he said. "Spot of food poisoning."

Amanda looked hopefully around the cabin. There was an empty seat next to a kid who had started throwing up during the take-off.

"Excuse me . . ." The guy beside her needed to go to the bathroom.

Amanda squeezed into the aisle.

"Everything okay with your husband?" an air hostess inquired.

"He's not my husband."

"Your friend, then." Her smile seemed baked on.

"Are there any spare seats in the next cabin?" Amanda asked.

"You wouldn't want to move, believe me," the hostess said. "There's a football team up there. The language! Most of the other passengers want to move."

Amanda fingered her identification, vacillating over whether to offer help.

"You get used to it," the hostess said. "Not much choice really."

The plane hit another air pocket and several children screamed. Amanda sat down again and closed her eyes. Hell was an eternal airflight, she thought.

Her companion returned, a damp face cloth pressed to his forehead. "I knew I shouldn't have eaten those prawns."

"I'm sure the prawns feel that way, too," Amanda joked.

He stared at her, disbelief vying with self-pity.

It dawned on Amanda that she was supposed to sympathize. He was a man, albeit a complete stranger, and she was a woman. Have breasts, will pamper. She removed a chocolate bar from the stash in her cabin bag and started munching.

There were still some loose ends, but the Petty case was looking solid, she reflected. They had questioned Mrs. Petty for two hours after she confessed. She admitted she'd taken a trip across the Tasman, ostensibly to see her daughter, as soon as Patrick Ryan had given her Bryce's address. He kept his spare key under a potted plant on his doorstep. It had been easy to borrow it and have a duplicate cut.

She'd entered Bryce's house expecting to find her clock. When it wasn't there, she left. The following week, she wrote to him from Melbourne. When she heard her clock had been sold, she decided to return to New Zealand and look for it. Unfortunately her husband had grown suspicious and found out she'd hired Patrick Ryan. He insisted on accompanying her to Wellington, and as soon as they'd arrived, he arranged for her to go and stay with Glenys. Not trusting her husband's intentions, Mrs. Petty went to Bryce's apartment on Monday, hoping to discover the whereabouts of her clock and convince her son to hand back the money. The rest was history.

After killing Bryce the following Wednesday, she had removed her bloody clothing in the shower box and changed back into the outfit she was wearing when she'd left Rotorua that morning. She carried the evidence with her as cabin luggage on the return flight from Wellington to Rotorua, then on the connection to Tauranga.

Her daughter didn't know a thing, she insisted. Late that night, after Glenys had gone to bed, she'd disposed of the bloody garments and towels. But she'd kept the gun, hiding it in a hatbox in her daughter's attic. In the days that followed, she decided to frame her husband for the murder, guessing he was a prime suspect. It had seemed like fair play, she said, after the way he'd tried to cheat her and Glenys.

Amanda was still puzzled by the female voice on the answer machine. She was almost certain that it was Glenys Petty, and wondered why she had called her brother that day. Had she known something? Was she somehow involved? Perhaps it would come out in court.

Repressing a surge of discomfort at the idea of the trial, Amanda unwrapped her second chocolate bar and reminded herself that Mrs. Petty had committed a murder and should be brought to justice. She would plead temporary insanity. The defense would argue she loved her son and was unhinged by his betrayal and cruelty. She might serve as little as four years, which seemed fair, somehow. Mrs. Petty's life sentence had been her marriage.

A chunk of chocolate clung to the roof of Amanda's mouth and she prised it off with her tongue. She should have suspected Mrs. Petty much sooner, she conceded inwardly. Mary Devine had been right when she implied Amanda's interpretation of the case data was skewed by a reluctance to see Mrs. Petty as a suspect. She had made assumptions instead of deductions. And, counting on her invisibility as an older woman, Mrs. Petty had almost gotten away with murder.

The plane lurched into another air pocket, and uttering a defeated moan, Amanda's companion leaned forward groping blindly for an airbag. Amanda opened it for him and patted his back when he was done. It was already the flight from hell, she reasoned. There was no need to get vomit on her shoes as well.

* * * * *

Janine Harrison met her at the luggage claim, her welcome so ecstatic Amanda wondered if she'd graduated from Pepsi to uppers.

Prattling about nothing in particular, she loaded Amanda's cases onto a trolley and led her from the terminal into a hazy soup of mist and exhaust fumes. Thoughtfully, she had parked the patrol car in the forbidden zone right outside the exit. Amanda got in the passenger side and kept her silence when Harrison flicked on the blue lights and forced a path through the crawling traffic.

"I can't believe it." She took the illegal shortcut across the airport tarmac to Moa Point. "*She* did it. Mrs. Ada Petty, housewife of the year."

"Good work on the husband's alibi," Amanda said.

"For what it was worth." Harrison gave a disgruntled snort. "I traced him in the end, you know. After he left the diocese, he was with someone called Chad from Cougar Escorts."

"Huge, hot and hunky?"

"That's what it says in the phone book." Harrison killed the blue lights and slowed down a little to enjoy the wild green ocean.

Amanda wound down her window, inviting the clean, cold salt air to sting her cheeks. "How's Sara?"

"Your friend Roseanne stayed out there with her last night. Oh, and by the way, your cat's pregnant."

"What?"

"Roseanne said to tell you. She took her to the vet yesterday and he said they're due any time."

They. Amanda closed her window. "Do you have a cat?"

Harrison shot her a suspicious look. "I've got tropical fish."

Amanda felt weak. "Did the vet say how many kittens?"

"They can't tell. But it will be at least four," Harrison assured her. "She's huge."

They both watched an albatross hanging motionless a few feet above the surf. A breaker crashed onto the road ahead of them, hurling spray against the windscreen. On the chill horizon the Cook Strait Ferry appeared wraithlike, a reminder of boats lost.

Amanda shivered. It was good to be back.

"Are you sure you don't want to drop by your place before we go up the coast?"

"No. I'd like to speak to Sara tonight."

"You want fast or comfortable?" Harrison inquired, suggestively revving the motor.

"Comfortable sounds good." Amanda reclined her seat a few notches. It was ninety minutes to Otaki. "Do you mind if I sleep?"

"Go right ahead. I can find my way."

As the miles went by, night swallowed the smoky apricot sky and Amanda's eyes grew heavy. In her mind, she floated out into that dark, soundless infinity as light and free as an atom.

CHAPTER EIGHTEEN

"Janine and I will go and buy dinner while you two catch up." Roseanne shoved wisps of fine brown hair into her disintegrating topknot. "What do you fancy? Fish and chips, burger, pizza, Chinese . . ."

"You choose," Amanda said.

Sara specified a crumbed schnapper fillet with tartar sauce. She seemed at ease, her feet encased in fluffy pink mules swinging lightly over the arm of her chair. "How was Melbourne?" she asked Amanda politely.

"Much warmer than Wellington," Amanda said. "And much bigger."

"I've only been to Sydney. For the Mardi Gras. It was wild."

"You're looking better." Amanda shifted to a personal focus.

Sara gazed into the crackling fire. "It's really nice of you and Roseanne to let me stay here. There's no one on the beach at this time of year. It's so peaceful."

Amanda agreed. "I like to come here in winter, too. It helps me get things into perspective."

"I've been doing some thinking," Sara said.

"And . . ." Amanda prompted gently.

"Last week all I wanted to do was hide somewhere and never go out again. I still feel like that a lot." She lowered her feet to the floor and reaching for the poker, she dallied with the fire. "Sometimes it all feels completely unreal, like it never happened, or it happened to a stranger, not to me. Then I start wondering if I really did lead Mel into thinking I wanted that stuff."

"Have you talked with Roseanne?"

"She's wonderful," Sara said. "She seems to know everything I'm feeling."

Are you going to press charges? Amanda yearned to ask. "I heard you've been pressured not to go ahead with the complaint."

"Women are saying Mel and Jolene will never get a fair trial." Sara sought Amanda's eyes, her own full of confusion. "What do you think . . . really?"

"I think the justice system isn't perfect. I think

Mel will serve time and Jolene will walk. But it's not your responsibility to protect them, Sara."

"I don't want them to get away with it," Sara said. "But I don't think I could live with seeing Jolene walking around while Mel is inside. It's just not fair."

"Let's be hypothetical for a moment," Amanda said. "What if you could have anything you wanted . . . any punishment?"

"I've thought about that, too," Sara said. "I'd want them both to admit what they did was wrong and apologize. Then I'd want them locked up."

"For how long?"

"I don't know . . . a year, maybe. Long enough so it hurts."

Amanda mentally sifted the evidence. There was a simple compromise open to them. "I can get you that kind of sentence," she said. "If we accept a plea on a lesser charge."

Plea bargaining was not a practice in New Zealand, but no prosecutor was going to complain over an undefended case. Jolene Ruth, with her investment in image, would definitely opt with an assault plea rather than standing trial for rape. And Mel had already admitted assault.

"If they both plead guilty to assault the case will go to court quickly and you'll only need to appear to give your statement," she said. "You won't be cross-examined."

"And you think they'll get the same sentence?"

"The prosecutor will recommend they do." Amanda extended her hands toward the flames. "As far as the apologies go . . ."

201

"I know." Sara gave a wistful smile. "They'll never do it."

"How do they sleep at night?" Roseanne said as they strolled along the beach much later. "I mean, they're women ... I can't believe it."

Amanda tied her scarf more securely about her neck and bounced her flashlight beam from side to side. The air was so cold it hurt her teeth, reminding her that her dental checkup was overdue. "Thanks for looking after Sara," she said.

"She'll be okay. I think it's the betrayal she finds hardest to deal with. Those women —" Roseanne expressed her disgust by kicking a piece of driftwood a few feet along the beach.

"How are you, anyway?" Amanda asked.

Roseanne laughed. "I'm back at work — just two days a week. I told them I can't make any promises. I'll see how it goes. While I think about it, did Janine tell you about your new cat?"

"I've seen kittens born before." Amanda tucked her arm into Roseanne's. She noticed her scent, a muskier fragrance than her usual floral. "You've changed your perfume," she remarked.

"This is what comes of hanging out with a detective — you can't have any secrets."

"Who is she?" Amanda inquired. The only time Roseanne changed her perfume was when she had a new lover.

"You met her at my party."

"That memorable evening ..." Amanda shuddered. "Not the silver cocktail dress?"

"No. Henry Dove, the writer." Roseanne was suddenly chattering. "She dropped by the next morning and helped me clean up. We'd never really talked before. It was great..."

Amanda felt an odd jolt recalling that for a passing moment she had contemplated a one-night stand with the attractive novelist. Don't say anything, she told herself.

"I like her a lot," Roseanne continued. "She's fun, she's interesting —" She broke off suddenly as though an appalling thought had crossed her mind. "You weren't... I mean, you and Henry..."

"Don't be ridiculous!" Amanda elbowed her. "I've got a girlfriend."

Roseanne leaned over and kissed her cheek. "Don't forget to tell *her* that, will you."

CHAPTER NINETEEN

Amanda let herself in through the kitchen door, dumped her luggage, turned on the lights and glanced around looking for the cats. They were both asleep on her armchair by the living room windows, apparently indifferent to the prospect of food.

"Hey, I'm home," Amanda told them.

Madam lifted her head briefly then covered it with a paw and went straight back to sleep. Her companion was comatose, her heaving stomach a portent of terrifying events to come.

Taking Roseanne's advice, Amanda hastily constructed a birthing box lined with paper and towels and placed this in tempting view inside the linen closet. Despite an attempt to interest Cosmos in the prospective nest, the hugely pregnant cat seemed unmoved. This was normal, Amanda supposed. Roseanne said she would start digging when it was time.

Imagining herself waking in the small hours to find a row of kittens on the pillow beside her, Amanda retreated upstairs. Something about her bedroom jarred. Catching a whiff of jasmine, she stared around, besieged suddenly with memories of last summer, the windows wide open, scents drifting in from her garden, Debby cradled against her.

Her eyes were drawn to the bathroom door. It was unlike her to leave the light on when she went to work, but she'd been absent-minded lately. Exasperated, she pulled off her clothes and tossed them into the laundry basket, conscious again of the smell of jasmine.

A shock of longing made her weak. Blood roared like an ocean in her ears. She could hardly breathe. Almost against her will, the nucleus of a decision seemed to be forming inside her. When finally it crystallized a long moment later, Amanda felt strangely disoriented.

Head spinning, she pushed open the bathroom door and stopped dead. Beyond a hazy wall of moisture, a familiar body reclined languidly in a jasmine-scented bubble bath.

"What took you so long?" Debby Daley stretched out a hand.

Amanda kissed the wet fingers and climbed into the tub, slowly immersing herself in the steaming water. "I guess you fed the cats," she said.

"All two and a half of them." Debby slid into her arms.

A few long, luscious kisses later, Amanda said, "I think we should continue this somewhere dry."

"Really?" Debby massaged her back with warm soapy hands, then started on her legs, her eyes never leaving Amanda's. "I missed you."

"I missed you too." Amanda pulled her to her feet and stood back a pace to gaze at her. The curves and hollows she remembered had altered subtly. "We've both shrunk," she concluded.

"There's a food shortage in Rwanda," Debby set about toweling her, nuzzling and biting as she went. "What's your excuse?"

"I was lovesick," Amanda held her still, staring into her eyes. "I never stopped thinking about you."

A blush rose from Debby's breasts to her cheeks. Her eyes dropped to Amanda's mouth. "I wanted you to say that."

Amanda's fingers were drawn inexorably to the secret places she most loved to explore. The tiny folds behind her ears, the indentations at the base of her spine, the delicate sinews at each wrist. Debby's skin felt hot from the bath, but wherever Amanda touched it goosebumps formed. Desire clawed at her gut. "I longed for you," she said.

Debby locked her hands behind Amanda's neck. "Show me how much."

Amanda swung her off the ground and carried her into the bedroom. It was almost perfect until they both started laughing.

"If only I'd filmed that!" Debby gasped, as Amanda tossed her onto the bed.

Pinning her shoulders down, Amanda kissed her into silence. Then, beset by an aching compulsion to be part of Debby's flesh, she found her way chaotically inside her, and they were suddenly gasping and biting and sweating as if they had only this moment to transcend their separation.

Later, they made love again, taking their time. Afterwards they lay on their backs, hands clasped, listening to their own breathing and the mysterious night sounds beyond their window.

Amanda slid off the plain gold band she wore on her little finger and held it out to Debby. Turning to her, she said, "I want to make promises to you."

Debby took the ring. "I'll hold you to them." Completely serious.

Amanda gathered her close. "I was hoping you'd say that."

A few of the publications of
THE NAIAD PRESS, INC.
P.O. Box 10543 • Tallahassee, Florida 32302
Phone (904) 539-5965
Toll-Free Order Number: 1-800-533-1973
Mail orders welcome. Please include 15% postage.

CHANGES by Jackie Calhoun. 208 pp. Involved romance and
relationships.   ISBN 1-56280-083-3   10.95

FAIR PLAY by Rose Beecham. 224 pp. 3rd Amanda Valentine
Mystery.   ISBN 1-56280-081-7   10.95

PAXTON COURT by Diane Salvatore. 256 pp. Erotic and wickedly
funny contemporary tale about the business of learning to live
together.   ISBN 1-56280-109-0   21.95

PAYBACK by Celia Cohen. 176 pp. A gripping thriller of romance,
revenge and betrayal.   ISBN 1-56280-084-1   10.95

THE BEACH AFFAIR by Barbara Johnson. 224 pp. Sizzling
summer romance/mystery/intrigue.   ISBN 1-56280-090-6   10.95

GETTING THERE by Robbi Sommers. 192 pp. Nobody does it
like Robbi!   ISBN 1-56280-099-X   10.95

FINAL CUT by Lisa Haddock. 208 pp. 2nd Carmen Ramirez
Mystery.   ISBN 1-56280-088-4   10.95

FLASHPOINT by Katherine V. Forrest. 256 pp. A Lesbian
blockbuster!   ISBN 1-56280-079-5   10.95

DAUGHTERS OF A CORAL DAWN by Katherine V. Forrest.
Audio Book — read by Jane Merrow.   ISBN 1-56280-110-4   16.95

CLAIRE OF THE MOON by Nicole Conn. Audio Book —Read
by Marianne Hyatt.   ISBN 1-56280-113-9   16.95

FOR LOVE AND FOR LIFE: INTIMATE PORTRAITS OF
LESBIAN COUPLES by Susan Johnson. 224 pp.
                                                  ISBN 1-56280-091-4   14.95

DEVOTION by Mindy Kaplan. 192 pp. See the movie — read
the book!   ISBN 1-56280-093-0   10.95

SOMEONE TO WATCH by Jaye Maiman. 272 pp. 4th Robin
Miller Mystery.   ISBN 1-56280-095-7   10.95

GREENER THAN GRASS by Jennifer Fulton. 208 pp. A young
woman — a stranger in her bed.   ISBN 1-56280-092-2   10.95

TRAVELS WITH DIANA HUNTER by Regine Sands. Erotic
lesbian romp. Audio Book (2 cassettes)   ISBN 1-56280-107-4   16.95

CABIN FEVER by Carol Schmidt. 256 pp. Sizzling suspense
and passion. ISBN 1-56280-089-1   10.95

THERE WILL BE NO GOODBYES by Laura DeHart Young. 192
pp. Romantic love, strength, and friendship. ISBN 1-56280-103-1   10.95

FAULTLINE by Sheila Ortiz Taylor. 144 pp. Joyous comic
lesbian novel. ISBN 1-56280-108-2   9.95

OPEN HOUSE by Pat Welch. 176 pp. 4th Helen Black Mystery.
ISBN 1-56280-102-3   10.95

ONCE MORE WITH FEELING by Peggy J. Herring. 240 pp.
Lighthearted, loving romantic adventure. ISBN 1-56280-089-2   10.95

FOREVER by Evelyn Kennedy. 224 pp. Passionate romance — love
overcoming all obstacles. ISBN 1-56280-094-9   10.95

WHISPERS by Kris Bruyer. 176 pp. Romantic ghost story
ISBN 1-56280-082-5   10.95

NIGHT SONGS by Penny Mickelbury. 224 pp. 2nd Gianna Maglione
Mystery. ISBN 1-56280-097-3   10.95

GETTING TO THE POINT by Teresa Stores. 256 pp. Classic
southern Lesbian novel. ISBN 1-56280-100-7   10.95

PAINTED MOON by Karin Kallmaker. 224 pp. Delicious
Kallmaker romance. ISBN 1-56280-075-2   10.95

THE MYSTERIOUS NAIAD edited by Katherine V. Forrest &
Barbara Grier. 320 pp. Love stories by Naiad Press authors.
ISBN 1-56280-074-4   14.95

DAUGHTERS OF A CORAL DAWN by Katherine V. Forrest.
240 pp. Tenth Anniversay Edition. ISBN 1-56280-104-X   10.95

BODY GUARD by Claire McNab. 208 pp. 6th Carol Ashton
Mystery. ISBN 1-56280-073-6   10.95

CACTUS LOVE by Lee Lynch. 192 pp. Stories by the beloved
storyteller. ISBN 1-56280-071-X   9.95

SECOND GUESS by Rose Beecham. 216 pp. 2nd Amanda Valentine
Mystery. ISBN 1-56280-069-8   9.95

THE SURE THING by Melissa Hartman. 208 pp. L.A. earthquake
romance. ISBN 1-56280-078-7   9.95

A RAGE OF MAIDENS by Lauren Wright Douglas. 240 pp. 6th Caitlin
Reece Mystery. ISBN 1-56280-068-X   10.95

TRIPLE EXPOSURE by Jackie Calhoun. 224 pp. Romantic drama
involving many characters. ISBN 1-56280-067-1   9.95

UP, UP AND AWAY by Catherine Ennis. 192 pp. Delightful
romance. ISBN 1-56280-065-5   9.95

PERSONAL ADS by Robbi Sommers. 176 pp. Sizzling short
stories. ISBN 1-56280-059-0   9.95

FLASHPOINT by Katherine V. Forrest. 256 pp. Lesbian
blockbuster!   ISBN 1-56280-043-4   22.95

CROSSWORDS by Penny Sumner. 256 pp. 2nd Victoria Cross
Mystery.   ISBN 1-56280-064-7   9.95

SWEET CHERRY WINE by Carol Schmidt. 224 pp. A novel of
suspense.   ISBN 1-56280-063-9   9.95

CERTAIN SMILES by Dorothy Tell. 160 pp. Erotic short stories.
                                      ISBN 1-56280-066-3   9.95

EDITED OUT by Lisa Haddock. 224 pp. 1st Carmen Ramirez
Mystery.   ISBN 1-56280-077-9   9.95

WEDNESDAY NIGHTS by Camarin Grae. 288 pp. Sexy
adventure.   ISBN 1-56280-060-4   10.95

SMOKEY O by Celia Cohen. 176 pp. Relationships on the
playing field.   ISBN 1-56280-057-4   9.95

KATHLEEN O'DONALD by Penny Hayes. 256 pp. Rose and
Kathleen find each other and employment in 1909 NYC.
                                      ISBN 1-56280-070-1   9.95

STAYING HOME by Elisabeth Nonas. 256 pp. Molly and Alix
want a baby . . . or do they?   ISBN 1-56280-076-0   10.95

TRUE LOVE by Jennifer Fulton. 240 pp. Six lesbians searching
for love in all the "right" places.   ISBN 1-56280-035-3   10.95

GARDENIAS WHERE THERE ARE NONE by Molleen Zanger.
176 pp. Why is Melanie inextricably drawn to the old house?
                                      ISBN 1-56280-056-6   9.95

KEEPING SECRETS by Penny Mickelbury. 208 pp. 1st Gianna
Maglione Mystery.   ISBN 1-56280-052-3   9.95

THE ROMANTIC NAIAD edited by Katherine V. Forrest &
Barbara Grier. 336 pp. Love stories by Naiad Press authors.
                                      ISBN 1-56280-054-X   14.95

UNDER MY SKIN by Jaye Maiman. 336 pp. 3rd Robin Miller
Mystery.   ISBN 1-56280-049-3.   10.95

STAY TOONED by Rhonda Dicksion. 144 pp. Cartoons — 1st
collection since *Lesbian Survival Manual.*   ISBN 1-56280-045-0   9.95

CAR POOL by Karin Kallmaker. 272pp. Lesbians on wheels
and then some!   ISBN 1-56280-048-5   10.95

NOT TELLING MOTHER: STORIES FROM A LIFE by Diane
Salvatore. 176 pp. Her 3rd novel.   ISBN 1-56280-044-2   9.95

GOBLIN MARKET by Lauren Wright Douglas. 240pp. 5th Caitlin
Reece Mystery.   ISBN 1-56280-047-7   10.95

LONG GOODBYES by Nikki Baker. 256 pp. 3rd Virginia Kelly
Mystery.   ISBN 1-56280-042-6   9.95

STONEHURST by Barbara Johnson. 176 pp. Passionate regency romance. ISBN 1-56280-024-8   10.95

INTRODUCING AMANDA VALENTINE by Rose Beecham. 256 pp. 1st Amanda Valentine Mystery. ISBN 1-56280-021-3   9.95

UNCERTAIN COMPANIONS by Robbi Sommers. 204 pp. Steamy, erotic novel. ISBN 1-56280-017-5   9.95

A TIGER'S HEART by Lauren W. Douglas. 240 pp. 4th Caitlin Reece Mystery. ISBN 1-56280-018-3   9.95

PAPERBACK ROMANCE by Karin Kallmaker. 256 pp. A delicious romance. ISBN 1-56280-019-1   9.95

MORTON RIVER VALLEY by Lee Lynch. 304 pp. Lee Lynch at her best! ISBN 1-56280-016-7   9.95

THE LAVENDER HOUSE MURDER by Nikki Baker. 224 pp. 2nd Virginia Kelly Mystery. ISBN 1-56280-012-4   9.95

PASSION BAY by Jennifer Fulton. 224 pp. Passionate romance, virgin beaches, tropical skies. ISBN 1-56280-028-0   10.95

STICKS AND STONES by Jackie Calhoun. 208 pp. Contemporary lesbian lives and loves. ISBN 1-56280-020-5   9.95
Audio Book (2 cassettes) ISBN 1-56280-106-6   16.95

DELIA IRONFOOT by Jeane Harris. 192 pp. Adventure for Delia and Beth in the Utah mountains. ISBN 1-56280-014-0   9.95

UNDER THE SOUTHERN CROSS by Claire McNab. 192 pp. Romantic nights Down Under. ISBN 1-56280-011-6   9.95

GRASSY FLATS by Penny Hayes. 256 pp. Lesbian romance in the '30s. ISBN 1-56280-010-8   9.95

A SINGULAR SPY by Amanda K. Williams. 192 pp. 3rd Madison McGuire Mystery. ISBN 1-56280-008-6   8.95

THE END OF APRIL by Penny Sumner. 240 pp. 1st Victoria Cross Mystery. ISBN 1-56280-007-8   8.95

HOUSTON TOWN by Deborah Powell. 208 pp. A Hollis Carpenter Mystery. ISBN 1-56280-006-X   8.95

KISS AND TELL by Robbi Sommers. 192 pp. Scorching stories by the author of *Pleasures*. ISBN 1-56280-005-1   10.95

STILL WATERS by Pat Welch. 208 pp. 2nd Helen Black Mystery. ISBN 0-941483-97-5   9.95

TO LOVE AGAIN by Evelyn Kennedy. 208 pp. Wildly romantic love story. ISBN 0-941483-85-1   9.95

IN THE GAME by Nikki Baker. 192 pp. 1st Virginia Kelly Mystery. ISBN 1-56280-004-3   9.95

AVALON by Mary Jane Jones. 256 pp. A Lesbian Arthurian romance. ISBN 0-941483-96-7   9.95

STRANDED by Camarin Grae. 320 pp. Entertaining, riveting
adventure.   ISBN 0-941483-99-1   9.95

THE DAUGHTERS OF ARTEMIS by Lauren Wright Douglas.
240 pp. 3rd Caitlin Reece Mystery.   ISBN 0-941483-95-9   9.95

CLEARWATER by Catherine Ennis. 176 pp. Romantic secrets
of a small Louisiana town.   ISBN 0-941483-65-7   8.95

THE HALLELUJAH MURDERS by Dorothy Tell. 176 pp. 2nd
Poppy Dillworth Mystery.   ISBN 0-941483-88-6   8.95

SECOND CHANCE by Jackie Calhoun. 256 pp. Contemporary
Lesbian lives and loves.   ISBN 0-941483-93-2   9.95

BENEDICTION by Diane Salvatore. 272 pp. Striking, contemporary romantic novel.   ISBN 0-941483-90-8   9.95

BLACK IRIS by Jeane Harris. 192 pp. Caroline's hidden past . . .
                                  ISBN 0-941483-68-1   8.95

TOUCHWOOD by Karin Kallmaker. 240 pp. Loving, May/
December romance.   ISBN 0-941483-76-2   9.95

COP OUT by Claire McNab. 208 pp. 4th Carol Ashton Mystery.
                                  ISBN 0-941483-84-3   9.95

THE BEVERLY MALIBU by Katherine V. Forrest. 288 pp. 3rd
Kate Delafield Mystery.   ISBN 0-941483-48-7   10.95

THAT OLD STUDEBAKER by Lee Lynch. 272 pp. Andy's affair
with Regina and her attachment to her beloved car.
                                  ISBN 0-941483-82-7   9.95

PASSION'S LEGACY by Lori Paige. 224 pp. Sarah is swept into
the arms of Augusta Pym in this delightful historical romance.
                                  ISBN 0-941483-81-9   8.95

THE PROVIDENCE FILE by Amanda Kyle Williams. 256 pp.
2nd Madison McGuire Mystery.   ISBN 0-941483-92-4   8.95

I LEFT MY HEART by Jaye Maiman. 320 pp. 1st Robin Miller
Mystery.   ISBN 0-941483-72-X   10.95

THE PRICE OF SALT by Patricia Highsmith (writing as Claire
Morgan). 288 pp. Classic lesbian novel, first issued in 1952 . . .
acknowledged by its author under her own, very famous, name.
                                  ISBN 1-56280-003-5   9.95

SIDE BY SIDE by Isabel Miller. 256 pp. From beloved author of
Patience and Sarah.   ISBN 0-941483-77-0   9.95

STAYING POWER: LONG TERM LESBIAN COUPLES by
Susan E. Johnson. 352 pp. Joys of coupledom. ISBN 0-941-483-75-4 14.95

SLICK by Camarin Grae. 304 pp. Exotic, erotic adventure.
                                  ISBN 0-941483-74-6   9.95

NINTH LIFE by Lauren Wright Douglas. 256 pp. 2nd Caitlin
Reece Mystery.   ISBN 0-941483-50-9   8.95

PLAYERS by Robbi Sommers. 192 pp. Sizzling, erotic novel.
ISBN 0-941483-73-8   9.95

MURDER AT RED ROOK RANCH by Dorothy Tell. 224 pp.
1st Poppy Dillworth Mystery.   ISBN 0-941483-80-0   8.95

LESBIAN SURVIVAL MANUAL by Rhonda Dicksion. 112 pp.
Cartoons!   ISBN 0-941483-71-1   8.95

A ROOM FULL OF WOMEN by Elisabeth Nonas. 256 pp.
Contemporary Lesbian lives.   ISBN 0-941483-69-X   9.95

THEME FOR DIVERSE INSTRUMENTS by Jane Rule. 208 pp.
Powerful romantic lesbian stories.   ISBN 0-941483-63-0   8.95

CLUB 12 by Amanda Kyle Williams. 288 pp. Espionage thriller
featuring a lesbian agent!   ISBN 0-941483-64-9   8.95

DEATH DOWN UNDER by Claire McNab. 240 pp. 3rd Carol
Ashton Mystery.   ISBN 0-941483-39-8   9.95

MONTANA FEATHERS by Penny Hayes. 256 pp. Vivian and
Elizabeth find love in frontier Montana.   ISBN 0-941483-61-4   8.95

LIFESTYLES by Jackie Calhoun. 224 pp. Contemporary Lesbian
lives and loves.   ISBN 0-941483-57-6   9.95

WILDERNESS TREK by Dorothy Tell. 192 pp. Six women on
vacation learning ''new'' skills.   ISBN 0-941483-60-6   8.95

MURDER BY THE BOOK by Pat Welch. 256 pp. 1st Helen
Black Mystery.   ISBN 0-941483-59-2   9.95

THERE'S SOMETHING I'VE BEEN MEANING TO TELL YOU
Ed. by Loralee MacPike. 288 pp. Gay men and lesbians coming out
to their children.   ISBN 0-941483-44-4   9.95

LIFTING BELLY by Gertrude Stein. Ed. by Rebecca Mark. 104 pp.
Erotic poetry.   ISBN 0-941483-51-7   10.95

AFTER THE FIRE by Jane Rule. 256 pp. Warm, human novel by
this incomparable author.   ISBN 0-941483-45-2   8.95

THREE WOMEN by March Hastings. 232 pp. Golden oldie. A
triangle among wealthy sophisticates.   ISBN 0-941483-43-6   8.95

PLEASURES by Robbi Sommers. 204 pp. Unprecedented
eroticism.   ISBN 0-941483-49-5   8.95

EDGEWISE by Camarin Grae. 372 pp. Spellbinding
adventure.   ISBN 0-941483-19-3   9.95

FATAL REUNION by Claire McNab. 224 pp. 2nd Carol Ashton
Mystery.   ISBN 0-941483-40-1   10.95

IN EVERY PORT by Karin Kallmaker. 228 pp. Jessica's sexy,
adventuresome travels.   ISBN 0-941483-37-7   9.95

OF LOVE AND GLORY by Evelyn Kennedy. 192 pp. Exciting
WWII romance.   ISBN 0-941483-32-0   10.95

CLICKING STONES by Nancy Tyler Glenn. 288 pp. Love
transcending time.   ISBN 0-941483-31-2   9.95

SOUTH OF THE LINE by Catherine Ennis. 216 pp. Civil War
adventure.   ISBN 0-941483-29-0   8.95

WOMAN PLUS WOMAN by Dolores Klaich. 300 pp. Supurb
Lesbian overview.   ISBN 0-941483-28-2   9.95

THE FINER GRAIN by Denise Ohio. 216 pp. Brilliant young
college lesbian novel.   ISBN 0-941483-11-8   8.95

OCTOBER OBSESSION by Meredith More. Josie's rich, secret
Lesbian life.   ISBN 0-941483-18-5   8.95

BEFORE STONEWALL: THE MAKING OF A GAY AND
LESBIAN COMMUNITY by Andrea Weiss & Greta Schiller.
96 pp., 25 illus.   ISBN 0-941483-20-7   7.95

OSTEN'S BAY by Zenobia N. Vole. 204 pp. Sizzling adventure
romance set on Bonaire.   ISBN 0-941483-15-0   8.95

LESSONS IN MURDER by Claire McNab. 216 pp. 1st Carol Ashton
Mystery.   ISBN 0-941483-14-2   9.95

YELLOWTHROAT by Penny Hayes. 240 pp. Margarita, bandit,
kidnaps Julia.   ISBN 0-941483-10-X   8.95

SAPPHISTRY: THE BOOK OF LESBIAN SEXUALITY by
Pat Califia. 3d edition, revised. 208 pp.   ISBN 0-941483-24-X   10.95

CHERISHED LOVE by Evelyn Kennedy. 192 pp. Erotic Lesbian
love story.   ISBN 0-941483-08-8   10.95

THE SECRET IN THE BIRD by Camarin Grae. 312 pp. Striking,
psychological suspense novel.   ISBN 0-941483-05-3   8.95

TO THE LIGHTNING by Catherine Ennis. 208 pp. Romantic
Lesbian 'Robinson Crusoe' adventure. ISBN 0-941483-06-1   8.95

DREAMS AND SWORDS by Katherine V. Forrest. 192 pp.
Romantic, erotic, imaginative stories. ISBN 0-941483-03-7   8.95

MEMORY BOARD by Jane Rule. 336 pp. Memorable novel
about an aging Lesbian couple.   ISBN 0-941483-02-9   10.95

THE ALWAYS ANONYMOUS BEAST by Lauren Wright Douglas.
224 pp. 1st Caitlin Reece Mystery.
                                      ISBN 0-941483-04-5   8.95

THE BLACK AND WHITE OF IT by Ann Allen Shockley.
144 pp. Short stories.   ISBN 0-930044-96-7   7.95

SAY JESUS AND COME TO ME by Ann Allen Shockley. 288
pp. Contemporary romance.   ISBN 0-930044-98-3   8.95

MURDER AT THE NIGHTWOOD BAR by Katherine V. Forrest.
240 pp. 2nd Kate Delafield Mystery.   ISBN 0-930044-92-4   10.95

WINGED DANCER by Camarin Grae. 228 pp. Erotic Lesbian
adventure story.   ISBN 0-930044-88-6   8.95

PAZ by Camarin Grae. 336 pp. Romantic Lesbian adventurer
with the power to change the world.   ISBN 0-930044-89-4   8.95

SOUL SNATCHER by Camarin Grae. 224 pp. A puzzle, an
adventure, a mystery — Lesbian romance.   ISBN 0-930044-90-8   8.95

THE LOVE OF GOOD WOMEN by Isabel Miller. 224 pp.
Long-awaited new novel by the author of the beloved *Patience
and Sarah.*   ISBN 0-930044-81-9   8.95

THE HOUSE AT PELHAM FALLS by Brenda Weathers. 240
pp. Suspenseful Lesbian ghost story.   ISBN 0-930044-79-7   7.95

HOME IN YOUR HANDS by Lee Lynch. 240 pp. More stories
from the author of *Old Dyke Tales.*   ISBN 0-930044-80-0   7.95

PEMBROKE PARK by Michelle Martin. 256 pp. Derring-do
and daring romance in Regency England.   ISBN 0-930044-77-0   7.95

THE LONG TRAIL by Penny Hayes. 248 pp. Vivid adventures
of two women in love in the old west.   ISBN 0-930044-76-2   8.95

AN EMERGENCE OF GREEN by Katherine V. Forrest. 288
pp. Powerful novel of sexual discovery.   ISBN 0-930044-69-X   10.95

THE LESBIAN PERIODICALS INDEX edited by Claire Potter.
432 pp. Author & subject index.   ISBN 0-930044-74-6   12.95

DESERT OF THE HEART by Jane Rule. 224 pp. A classic;
basis for the movie *Desert Hearts.*   ISBN 0-930044-73-8   10.95

TORCHLIGHT TO VALHALLA by Gale Wilhelm. 128 pp.
Classic novel by a great Lesbian writer.   ISBN 0-930044-68-1   7.95

LESBIAN NUNS: BREAKING SILENCE edited by Rosemary
Curb and Nancy Manahan. 432 pp. Unprecedented autobiographies
of religious life.   ISBN 0-930044-62-2   9.95

THE SWASHBUCKLER by Lee Lynch. 288 pp. Colorful novel
set in Greenwich Village in the sixties.   ISBN 0-930044-66-5   8.95

SEX VARIANT WOMEN IN LITERATURE by Jeannette
Howard Foster. 448 pp. Literary history.   ISBN 0-930044-65-7   8.95

A HOT-EYED MODERATE by Jane Rule. 252 pp. Hard-hitting
essays on gay life; writing; art.   ISBN 0-930044-57-6   7.95

AMATEUR CITY by Katherine V. Forrest. 224 pp. 1st Kate
Delafield Mystery.   ISBN 0-930044-55-X   10.95

THE SOPHIE HOROWITZ STORY by Sarah Schulman. 176 pp.
Engaging novel of madcap intrigue.   ISBN 0-930044-54-1   7.95

These are just a few of the many Naiad Press titles — we are the oldest and
largest lesbian/feminist publishing company in the world. Please request a
complete catalog. We offer personal service; we encourage and welcome
direct mail orders from individuals who have limited access to bookstores
carrying our publications.